Bag Man

a Leathan Wilkey novella

Simon Cann

Coombe
Hill
Publishing

Published by Coombe Hill Publishing
33 Melrose Gardens
New Malden
Surrey KT3 3HQ
United Kingdom
coombehillpublishing.com

ISBN: 9781910398166 (paperback)
ISBN: 9781910398173 (ePub)

A big thank you to Cathleen Small for her editorial input.

18 March 2017

one

"I don't trust—"

Claude cut across me before I could finish my sentence. "You don't trust her, she doesn't trust you, and I don't trust either of you. So we're all even." He sucked on his cigar, then picked up his espresso cup with his other hand, holding the small lump of white porcelain delicately between his thick thumb and stubby middle finger as he pointed at me—the cup becoming a makeshift finger. "Are you happy now?"

"It's a trap."

Claude took a sip of espresso and returned his cup to its saucer. "Possibly." As the hand with his cup lowered, his other raised itself like a seesaw bringing up his cigar. He sucked the burning leaves. "Probably."

The fat man seemed happy to let the conversation dry up. He stared at his cigar, his look one of contemplation in the way one might contemplate a vintage wine.

The weather in Paris had turned. The last few crisp autumnal days had been banished, being replaced by gray mornings with biting wind whipping off la Seine, and frequent heavy showers. The city was moving quickly, desperate to get inside before it rained again. Again. Getting wet wasn't the problem—the problem was being wet when the wind picked up.

Claude and I stood by the waist-high table outside the café. Outside: Claude's one begrudging concession to the legislation banning smoking inside. I barely knew him, we'd only spoken once before, but I knew Claude firmly believed the legislation banning smoking inside was contrary to the principles of *liberté, égalité, fraternité*, not to mention all the statutes in the French, European, and United Nations corpus of legislation that had been written since the founding of the Republic.

But for the fat man, the inconvenience was not being outside—I suspected it was standing. His battered raincoat, misbuttoned and a shade somewhere between gray and brown, bore testament to meals eaten since the weather turned and meals eaten during the previous years' rainy seasons. His conversation wasn't so much talk as gesticulation, and unless he was sitting, he was too much of a target as his food spilled from his fast-moving hand.

"Your choice. Do you want the job or not?" asked Claude. "Do the job, take a risk, get paid. Or walk away and I'll find someone else. Do the job well, and maybe there's more work for you."

"Get killed and you'll organize my funeral?" I asked, instinctively rubbing my arms for warmth.

He snorted. "You're funny for an Englishman."

"Probably because I'm Scottish," I muttered. But I suspected Claude knew that my father was Scottish and my mother French. He was probably only sniping because he was getting bored by my reluctance to simply agree to accept the job. "Who's the client?" I asked.

"She's either a saint or a devil, depending on who you believe. If you're concerned about business, then Gabriela Carvalho turned around a failing Brazilian mining company and made it a global player. In so doing, she became a feminist icon—mother and CEO. If you worry about polar bears, then she's the devil slashing and burning her way through the Amazon jungle to satisfy her own greed."

Claude sipped his espresso, apparently satisfied that I now had sufficient information.

"Why me?" I asked.

Claude contemplated the question—a Parisian philosopher weighing the nature of the matter. "Why you, Leathan Wilkey? Or why you and not the cops or some private army?"

"Both, I guess."

"You, and not the cops, because Gabriela Carvalho doesn't want the cops involved. She doesn't trust them and she doesn't want the publicity. If it gets known that she paid a ransom for her kid, that will show there was a weakness in her security and that she has a vulnerability. Wherever she goes, they'll be lining up to grab the kid again."

"Then she's got security? So why me?"

"You, Leathan, because..." He stared into the distance. "Because."

"Because?"

"Because they need someone with local knowledge who speaks the language."

"There are people who know more about Paris," I said. "I've only been here for six weeks."

Claude stubbed out his cigar and lit another. It came from the same pack, but he savored the first draw as if this were some new and exotic pleasure he had never previously enjoyed. "My friend the lawyer recommended you. He was returning the favor—he said you got him hired and his client said good things about you. He said you're good at this sort of thing."

"What sort of thing is that?" I asked. A gust of wind blew, bringing with it a sheet of moisture that wasn't quite rain.

The muscles in Claude's flabby face tightened slightly. "Kids, families, thinking on your feet, giving a shit, sorting stuff out..." said Claude, not giving emphasis to any particular aspect. He gripped the table and faced me directly, the tone of his voice dropped. "She needs your help, Leathan. Will you meet her?"

two

I stepped out of the elevator onto a sea of thick carpet, with muted tones on the walls and fittings that suggested they were—although they clearly weren't—gold. The room wasn't hard to find; there were only a few doors reinforcing the message that this was where the money stayed when it was visiting Paris.

In the few weeks I'd been living in Paris on a more permanent basis, I'd been cautious to ensure that I wasn't at a given location at a given time and that I didn't go from point A to point B directly. If I was predictable, if my movements were known in advance, then the reason I left London—an angry gang of Bulgarian people traffickers—would find it easier to locate me. But if I kept moving, then I was a needle in a stack of other needles.

However, there was a kid in danger, and I figured a bunch of Bulgarian thugs would look out of place in one of Paris' most expensive hotels. Added to which, this hotel wasn't where you'd lure someone if your intent were to harm them.

Then again, maybe the Bulgarians were smarter than I thought. Maybe they had figured that in an upmarket hotel I would walk straight in, confident that I was safe.

As I negotiated with Claude, I did a quick calculation in my head—a balance of risks coupled with an assessment of possibilities and probabilities—and agreed that I would meet Gabriela Carvalho, the chief executive of Saint Joseph Mining Company. And that was the full extent of what I had agreed to. Well, I also agreed that I would get a cab directly to her hotel—there was a kidnapped kid and a lack of time.

The woman who answered the door had a phone held firmly against her left ear. She was talking forcefully, although not loudly, in a language I didn't completely recognize. My guess was Portuguese. A guess that wasn't so much based on my knowledge of languages, but more on the fact that Claude had told me Gabriela Carvalho was Brazilian and Saint Joseph Mining Company was based in Brazil.

She was short, maybe five four, but broad. Not heavy, but wide, and dressed in a functional light brown suit that offset her olive skin and bleached hair, which had taken on a yellow hue under the artificial light. She continued her conversation without pause; her only communication with me was to make eye contact and then flick her eyes into the room as if commanding me to enter. I stepped across the threshold, and she shut the door behind me before she led me through to a reception room.

It was a large, impractical space, rather than a room with a designed function.

In the middle there were three low sofas with a low table. There was a large television on a wall, but it was positioned so it would be uncomfortable to watch while sitting on any of the sofas. A narrow and unnecessarily small table by a wall was laid several bottles of water and some clean glasses. In each of the two side walls there were two doors, giving the room the feeling of a train station rather than a place where you might sit and relax. The fourth wall—the outside wall—had full-length windows with dark glass that looked over the city but somehow managed not to see any of the grace of the metropolis.

My host's conversation on her phone continued, with her voice becoming louder and more forceful. She hung up but gripped her phone in her hand, which she now held at waist height as she looked down at the screen, swiping away messages.

"Leathan," she said in an accent that suggested South American heritage. Her complexion, her slightly wavy hair tied back but still fighting for both its freedom and its natural dark color, told me her heritage was South American but likely had its roots in Europe. Her first words that were not my name were in French. Like me, she had a command of the language and an accent. "Thank you for coming at such short notice."

"I'm pleased to meet you, Miss Carvalho."

That broke her focus on her screen. She looked up, smiled, then returned her eyes to the electronic device as she spoke. "I'm sorry, I'm not Gabriela—and please call her Gabriela—I'm Beatriz Marques, her assistant."

"I'm sorry," I stumbled, "I'm here to see Miss...I mean, Gabriela."

Beatriz, the assistant with a command of her own language and French, not to mention a command of her phone, tutted, tapped forcefully on the screen, remained motionless watching the device, and then looked up, giving a small smile before returning her gaze to her phone and responding. "She's not here."

Something about the shift in my demeanor must have given away my reaction, because without looking at me she answered the question I silently voiced. Or rather, she gave me the answer to the ultimate question I would have asked if she had engaged me in conversation. She might call herself an assistant, but I was beginning to suspect that mind reading was within her job description.

"It's important that we give no indication that anything is wrong," she said, again lifting her eyes from her screen, but this time fixing her gaze on me. The phone beeped, but Beatriz kept her eyes locked on mine. "Do you understand? Gabriela is continuing as if nothing is wrong. We must do the same."

Before I could answer, she held up a finger as if silencing me, and lifted the phone to her ear. I could pick up a few words: Tuesday, meeting, Venice, no, New York, dinner, no, breakfast. I suspected the language being spoken was Dutch, but that was just a guess. It was another language in which I could order a beer and say thank you, and that was enough for me.

My only hint that the call had ended was that Beatriz dropped her finger holding me silent. Her other hand held the phone, but now it was a few inches in front and to the right of her face.

A man walked in, holding a small but well-filled backpack by its strap. Like the assistant he had an olive-like complexion and seemed to be in his thirties. Where she was short, he was tall, but he had the same width, and while his dark suit was roughly the right size for him, something in the way he carried himself suggested he was dressed this way to camouflage his true intent. Where her hair was unkempt but tied back, his was straight and cut short, and retained its natural near-black tone.

Neither Beatriz nor this man acknowledged each other as he moved silently across the room and sat on the farther sofa.

When she continued speaking, Beatriz spoke in English. "This is Matheus Santos. He's in charge of Gabriela's security—he will tell you what to do." She indicated that I should sit on the sofa across from the man, and by the time I looked back to her she was talking on her phone.

Santos half stood and half reached a hand to shake as I sat. His focus was directed to the assistant. He said something, I guessed in Portuguese.

Beatriz made a comment that felt affirmative, then pulled out a second identical phone while continuing her conversation on the first.

The security man faced me directly, the backpack on his lap. He looked down to the backpack, then up to me, held my gaze, and just at the point it was becoming uncomfortable, broke to look back to his lap. When he spoke, his English was heavily accented. "Take the bag. Give it to the nasty man. Bring back the kid." He held out the backpack toward me.

"Your father was French and your mother English?" said the assistant.

I lifted my hands to take the backpack offered by Matheus and stopped, realizing the question from Beatriz had been directed at me. The second phone was now clamped to her other ear; the first phone was held out as she flicked through her messages.

"Scottish father, French mother," I said to the assistant, taking the bag from the security man.

She said something, then looked toward me, eyeing me in the way a farmer would consider a cow at the market. She said something more into the second phone as her eyes left me and moved back to her first phone.

The bag pushed into my hands and instinctively I took it, feeling the weight as I accepted it from Matheus Santos. "Is that...? Can I...?" I said to Beatriz. "I'd like to..."

She ended the call and returned the second phone directly to her jacket pocket. "Gabriela says thank you for your help."

"Can I speak with her?"

"I thought you understood," said Beatriz, slowly and in English. "Gabriela cannot let there be any suggestion of a problem." Matheus nodded as she spoke. "And Matheus will tell you what to do."

Before I could form a word, she was back on her phone.

Matheus fixed me with his stare and repeated in his heavily accented English. "Take the bag. Give it to the nasty man. Bring back the kid." He waited, not breaking his stare. "Understand?"

"I'd like to talk with..." I began.

"No time," said the personal security man. "You have a phone?"

I nodded.

"Give me." He held out a hand and put his other hand into a jacket pocket, pulling out a cheap phone. "Take this. They will give you instructions on this. You answer, they say, you go." He pulled my phone away and pushed his phone into my hands before I could explain that I hadn't agreed to do anything.

There was the sound of sobbing from a room at the side. Without breaking her conversation, Beatriz strode in the direction of the oddly high-pitched distraction.

"The nanny," said Matheus, seemingly not sure if his English vocabulary was correct. "Woman who look after Guilherme..."

"There's a nanny?" I asked, trying to keep the surprise out of my voice. As I understood from the few facts Claude had offered, Gabriela Carvalho styled herself as mother of Guilherme, her seven-year-old she was raising single-handedly, and CEO of Saint Joseph Mining Company. Both roles were equally important to what, I guessed, you would call her *brand*.

"Luiza. Very upset. Says it's her fault." I suspected he would have liked to explain to me exactly how it was her fault.

I waited to see if he would elaborate.

"Big secret," said Matheus. "No internet, no newspaper. We say she is..." He mimed typing.

There was a conversation in the other room. While I couldn't translate, I could recognize the assistant's voice. The other voice was high and squeaky—almost comically high and squeaky. Beatriz returned, rolling her eyes at Matheus without interrupting her conversation on the phone. She ignored the few words that were squeaked behind her.

I became aware of the weight on my lap—it felt like about twenty pounds—and shifted the backpack to my side.

"Don't open it. Don't look inside," said the other man. "Is..." he held up his hand as if it were the sun shining, "beep, beep, beep."

"GPS," I offered. "A tracker?"

He nodded. "So we know where the money is."

"Isn't that risky?"

A shake of his head. "When Guilherme is safe—safe first—we want to get money back." Then for emphasis, "Guilherme safe first."

I tried to figure how to ask whether a tracker would endanger Guilherme—maybe his kidnappers would feel that we weren't being straight—but I was distracted by the sound of the door to the suite opening. A younger guy walked into the room. Slimmer than Matheus and better dressed, or at least his clothes fit him better.

Matheus turned to face him and said something. The younger man replied, indicating toward himself and looking between Matheus and Beatriz. The woman gave a command; the tone was definite. The younger man then passed something to Matheus, said a few words, and left. His footsteps where heavier than when he arrived, and the closing of the door was louder than when he entered.

"Gabriela's driver," said Matheus. "Mister Pierre Alvaréz thinks he should carry the money, but his job is to be there when the boss needs to be driven."

"If he wants," I began.

The other man snorted. "He has gel for his hands. You know—for germs."

"Antibacterial," I offered. The other man nodded—I wasn't sure whether he was agreeing or if this was something he did when a foreign word had too many syllables.

"He has special cleaner for his face and always keeps his clothes clean. We check into a hotel, his first call is for laundry. No. I'm relying on you." He held something toward me. Reflexively, I held out my hand and he dropped a car key into my palm. "Silver Audi downstairs. They call, you drive. Give the bag to the nasty man. Bring back Guilherme."

three

The silver Audi was small and boxy. I recognized it as the car that was intended for me because it was silver, it didn't have a chauffeur, and there was a zero missing from the price tag when compared to the other cars at the front of the hotel. This was the car the other residents of the hotel wouldn't even give to their staff.

I checked the trunk—there was no dead body—made sure the engine turned over, and looked to see that I had fuel. As I tried to figure out the dials, the phone rang. "Yeah," I said. I chose English, but the word is comprehensible by speakers of most European languages.

There was a brief pause. There was a sigh and then some muffled words in French. "Have you got the money?"

"Yeah." Instinctively I put my hand on the backpack on the passenger seat.

"Place de la Concorde. Keep circling; we'll tell you where next." And the call ended.

I smiled to myself as I pulled back into the traffic. Place de la Concorde was something of an obvious place to send me. The largest public square in Paris, which worked as a huge traffic interchange. But despite the cold and frequent rain, it was also a tourist magnet. Situated at the end of Avenue des Champs-Élysées, looking toward l'Arc de Triomphe in one direction and Musée du Louvre in the other, it was a perfect place for someone to stay totally inconspicuous while watching a silver car driving around.

As I started my second loop of the square the phone rang again. "Yeah."

I spent the next two hours being directed around Paris, taking in some of the city's tourist sites, many of its backstreets, but mostly I saw its traffic jams in the rain. Maybe the guys who were directing me were professionals and knew what they were doing. Maybe they were buying time. Maybe they had seen this in a movie. Whatever the case, I could see no logic, but then I was sent to a public parking lot. "Second level, red VW. Leave your phone and leave the key in the ignition."

I found the red VW and pulled the silver Audi into the space across from the other car. I left the key in the ignition, left the phone Matheus Santos had given me on the driver's seat, and didn't lock the car.

All I took was the backpack.

The VW was warm inside, like someone had been driving it and had just parked. I got out of the car and felt the hood—it was still warm. This felt like a step in the plan that had been added since I started driving around. A plan that was being made up as they went along.

The key was in the VW's ignition, and a new but equally cheap phone was on the passenger seat. As I sat, the phone began to ring. "Pay the parking, then head north."

"Where's the kid?" I asked. The caller had already hung up.

The VW drove just like the Audi, which shouldn't have been surprising—the cars were basically the same, same chassis, same engine, same manufacturer, just different badges. The only real difference was that this had a GPS unit stuck to the windshield. The power cable trailed across the dashboard and I presumed found its way to the cigarette lighter.

The third call gave a clear instruction. "Go where the GPS takes you."

It was now a while after 2 PM. The day had lost whatever heat it ever had, and on this early winter day in the northern hemisphere, the light was weak. Not that the cloud cover was helping.

I drove west. I wasn't sure where I was going. I was following the GPS, which had been programmed with only one location, and that location was a set of coordinates— longitude and latitude rather than a specific place.

The GPS directed me into Bois de Boulogne, the large public park on the west of the city, and after a few minutes ordered me off the main highway and onto a smaller road. I guessed that in summer this place would be packed, but this side road was nearly empty. The GPS turned me to the right again, pushing me into the woods along what was little more than a narrow track with a thin layer of blacktop that had worn gray.

At the end of the track there was a large hut. It had probably once been a café or a refreshment stand. In summer it might still be, but now it was just a closed hut. There wasn't so much a parking lot, but more of a turning circle with another even smaller track leading off. One car was parked in the turning circle. Local. Unflashy. Probably a dog walker or an exercise fiend.

I pulled the VW to a halt and the phone rang. "Walk. Take the other track."

"Do you mean...?" I began, but he hung up.

four

The rain had stopped, but as I got out of the car I felt the bite of the wind coming of la Seine, which was a few hundred yards away. The park is called Bois de Boulogne. Bois. Bois translates as woods. And there were many, many trees, but none of them seemed to offer any protection against the wind. All they did was obscure any chance I had of seeing what I was walking into.

I slung the backpack from one shoulder and followed the smaller track. At a guess this was originally a firebreak. The gate blocking the access to vehicles—functional steel tubing, a hinge on one side and a padlock on the other—told me it now had a second function as a service road. I walked around the gate and followed the track between the trees.

The trees thinned giving me a view of a black Land Cruiser with tinted windows. There was a guy to the left with another to the right, both semi-camouflaged by their surroundings, but now clear. I let my gaze scan across my surroundings, taking in as much detail as I could, while realizing they had been aware of me long before I had seen anything.

The Land Cruiser's driver door opened, and a man stepped out, wearing a business suit without a tie. He shut the car door, fastened the top button of his jacket—seemingly the only measure to acknowledge the temperature—and then turned to me. I was about thirty yards off when he held up his hand, stopping me.

He continued walking toward me. Casually. Walking like this wasn't even a business meeting for him. Despite the cold, walking like he was going out to get lunch on a warm spring day.

As he got close I became aware of the sound of feet behind me, the other two guys forming an equilateral triangle with the suited third. Up close, the semi-camouflage for the other two was jeans and scruffy jackets. Both looked to their suited colleague for direction. Where he was measured in his movements, these two were twitching. Neither could or would stand still.

I checked again; both were holding guns.

Holding pistols and twitching.

"Where's the kid?" I asked the suited leader.

For the first time his face showed some emotion—a half smile. "Money," he said, holding out a hand and snapping his fingers. From one word I recognized him as French.

"I want to see Guilherme," I said. The feet shuffled behind me with more agitation.

"And I want..." He paused. His eyes flicked to the right, there was a shuffling of feet, and my arm was grabbed. Cold metal pressed against my temple.

The third man pulled the backpack from my shoulder and took the offering to his master like a faithful hunting dog.

"Where's Guilherme?" I asked, trying not to stare at the backpack as I thought about the tracker Matheus had planted. My arm was pulled tighter and the pistol jabbed hard into my cheek.

I could have sworn the guy in the suit shrugged as he started to unzip the backpack that his faithful retriever was holding for him.

"The kid," I said and felt a punch land in my kidneys.

"Shh," said the suited guy, otherwise ignoring my plight as I tried to stifle the involuntary shout I made. "This is a place of peace and tranquility. Listen to the birds sing."

The birds had been smart and had flown south months ago. I righted myself and watched as he started to look in the backpack. He pulled out a small bundle of bills held together by an elastic band. He riffled through the bills, looked to me, and then riffled through the bills again.

The fist from the scruffy guy beside me hit me in the gut this time. When I righted myself, the suited man was standing directly in front of me, riffling the stack of bills. "This?"

I searched my mind for a smart explanation about a tracker. I tried to find some way to tell him it was good for me and good for him—you know, just in case I lost the backpack on my way over.

The next punch distracted me. It hurt less, but I didn't want my assailant to realize that, so I made sure my audio commentary told him he had been effective, and I reinforced the message by bending double.

The suited man made a clicking sound; an instruction to the man beside me. My hair was grabbed and I was pulled up straight. "Where's the kid?" I asked.

He held the stack of cash between his thumb and forefinger. "This? For the kid?"

"That was the deal. Where is he?"

He riffled through the stack of bills, holding the stack in my line of vision but not too close—I was meant to see what he was doing. He riffled, then looked up at me, questioning, and then riffled again. "Well?"

I said nothing. I couldn't see any sign of a tracker.

He riffled again, looked questioningly at me again, and waited.

"Do that again," I said.

He riffled.

"Shit," I muttered, finally understanding the point he was trying to make. Finally understanding what he had been showing me as he riffled the bills.

He considered my assessment, then flicked his eyes to my assailant.

Solid metal slammed into the side of my head, and a fist made contact with my gut. I remember falling but not landing.

five

I was on the ground—a thin layer of blacktop, laid badly over rough ground without proper foundations. A thin layer of blacktop still wet from the rain.

The suited man and his two scruffy followers were talking. Or rather, he seemed to be trying to think while they talked, and I was beginning to suspect they didn't have my best interests at heart. The question wasn't so much whether I lived, but more where I died—it might be noticed if I was shot here, although a car driven into the woods might give some protection—and then there was also the issue of how quickly they needed me to be found. Apparently there was no point in killing me if the message it sent wasn't received.

"Here. Now," said one of the two scruffs, cocking his pistol.

The suited man sighed. "Patience."

I let my eyes stay closed—no need to let them know I was conscious—and listened. There was a vehicle, moving swiftly and coming in our direction from the other end of the track.

The tone of their voices changed—they had become aware of the vehicle. The suited man said something hurriedly, and there was the sound of feet moving. I remained still but opened an eye. The two scruffs had gone left and right, and the suited man was heading toward the Land Cruiser. Beyond the vehicle, the source of the panic was a dark blue Mercedes SUV—a box with a three-pointed star slapped on the front—skidding to a halt with the passenger door already open.

As the driver's door began to open, there was a shot. I couldn't tell whether it was aimed at the Mercedes or from the Mercedes. All I knew was that it wasn't aimed at me and that I felt a need not to be lying on the road.

There were three more shots. Each a slightly different pitch, none with an obvious source or destination.

I got to my feet, or at least I got to a squatting position—I didn't need to show more body mass than was necessary if people wanted targets—and looked. The closer trees were thinner—the farther trees were more densely packed. I headed for them, running fast and trying to keep low.

There were more shots and a cry of pain. My eyes followed the sound, and I saw one of the scruffs holding himself. His head turned and his eyes met mine. There was a moment of recognition, and I broke contact to focus on my destination, still maybe thirty yards away but closing fast. He shouted. I ignored him and kept running, pushing myself harder. Faster. The blood pumping and any notion that I might be in pain temporarily forgotten.

Another shout and then a shot. It felt close. I couldn't be sure how close, but it was unquestionably aimed at me, or at least toward me. A second shot, then a third, and I reached the trees, hearing a fourth and a fifth shot bury themselves in the wood as I kept running.

Some way into the trees I slowed and looked back. There were four figures who seemed to have stopped shooting each other.

The man who had got out of the Mercedes SUV—who from a distance looked very much like Matheus Santos, Gabriela Carvalho's head of security—was up at the black Land Cruiser. It seemed he had all the doors, including the back door, open and was now shouting at the man who had taken the money from me.

I turned away and continued running.

six

I hauled myself out of the cab, feeling my new bruises, and dropped a €50 bill for the driver. "Merci, monsieur."

It was the same café where we had met a few hours earlier. I found Claude sitting at a table inside. His raincoat was recognizable in among the other coats hanging on a rack on the other side of the room.

"Leathan, Leathan," said the fat man, half standing and knocking his coffee—his earlier espresso having been exchanged for a filter coffee that slopped out of its mug. He held his arms out as if he were going to hug me. His inability to stand up straight and get out from behind the table assured me I would avoid his embrace. With one hand he beckoned a waiter. "Coffee, Leathan? Something to eat?"

The waiter reached us. "Just a coffee, please."

We sat; the wooden chair offered little comfort and no relief for my bruises, but it was good to be inside and not lying on wet blacktop. The café might have been basic in its decoration—stripped wood floor, white render walls—but it was warm. "So the kid's back in his maternal embrace and all is right in the world?" The smile under his layers of blubber wasn't a fake—this was the real deal; he was even smiling with his eyes.

"What the fuck did you send me into, Claude?"

His face fell, the blubber wobbling as the muscles holding the smile released. "What are you talking about, Leathan?"

"Don't…" I began, and stopped as the waiter returned with my coffee.

Claude had managed to form his face into some sort of mask of concern. Or maybe he was concerned. He took a sip of his coffee and raised his eyebrows.

I didn't give him the satisfaction of an explanation. I sat and waited. He blinked first. "I've been here all day—it was too wet to go walking, so I came inside. I haven't heard anything from Gabriela Carvalho..." He saw the look cross my face. "Gabriela Carvalho—or any of her people—since I last saw you. So please, Leathan, tell me what happened."

I tried to calibrate whether Claude was part of the problem, part of the solution, or just my confessor here to give me absolution for perhaps being part of Guilherme Carvalho's death.

"They sent me with fake cash," I said.

"Good fake or bad fake?" asked Claude.

"Does it matter? They sent me to a ransom exchange with fake cash and didn't tell me I had fake cash. Who do you think takes the first bullet when there's fake cash?"

Claude sighed his agreement to my basic proposition.

"And as I was trying to exchange this cash—which I had just found out was fake—they came in, all guns blazing."

"They?" asked Claude without belligerence.

It was my turn to sigh and shrug. "I can't be completely certain—there were bullets flying everywhere, and I was running—but the guy who came in looked like Matheus Santos, Gabriela's security, and the one who gave me the currency produced on a laser printer."

"Bad fake," muttered Claude quietly under his breath. His face brightened. "So they sent you with fakes, but they knew there would be a problem and tried to step in."

I snorted. "From the way they behaved, they just wanted to grab the kid. This was an attempt to get the kid without paying the ransom. I was just there to draw the fire."

Claude went to respond but paused, the folds of skin in his face twitching as he seemed to have a silent conversation with himself. Before he could finish, I continued. "The kid wasn't there."

He met my eyes, and I nodded. A simple exchange by which we both acknowledged that these things aren't always that simple—the risks are high when bringing a hostage to a location. The events of less than an hour ago amply demonstrated why the kidnappers would have been smart not to bring Guilherme.

"I'm not explaining this well," I said. "The kid wasn't there. I get that. But it was like these guys didn't know who the kid was. They behaved as if they were just there to rob me. I don't think they've actually got the kid."

Claude sensed my anger was ebbing. He half shrugged. "You did what was asked, you'll get paid."

"This isn't about the money." I felt the anger return and my volume increase.

Claude waited. The movement of his head was an all-encompassing gesture to be placatory and to suggest there was little need to shout.

"Too much is wrong. There's a kid who's being held hostage, and there's a bunch of incompetents running around while his mother keeps up the public image. The kid's in danger, and I want to talk to Gabriela."

"You'll get your money. Nothing more is going to happen today, so go and have a beer, find a woman, and have a bath—but not in that order. You look like you need a wash first."

"I need a wash. I need a new phone…" Claude's fat brow creased. "They—Gabriela's security—took my phone. But I need to talk to Gabriela. I've been shot at, so I think I'm due an explanation, and I'm the only one who actually seems to care about this kid's welfare."

"Look," said Claude. He reached into his pocket and pulled out a pad and a stubby pencil. He scribbled something and before tearing out the page and handing it to me. "Go and see Nazim. That's his address—it's about ten minutes' walk. He runs one of those electronics shops. Tell him I sent you, and he'll give you a new phone. It'll be secondhand, but he'll give you a decent one. And while you're getting a new phone, I'll make some calls and find out what happened."

seven

The light had left the day as I returned to the café with my new secondhand phone from Nazim. Claude was at the table where, as far as I could tell, he had taken up residence a few moments after I left him that morning when we had talked outside so he could smoke. Now it seemed that warmth, electric light, food, and a seat trumped his need for a cigar.

He seemed concerned, maybe conciliatory, as I sat. "You need to eat, Leathan. Let me order—"

"I'm fine."

"You should—"

"Really, Claude. I just want to..." I sighed. I wasn't quite sure what I wanted. Was I more concerned about the situation I'd be thrown into or was I more concerned about the kid? Or was it a something of both?

"I've spoken to Miss Carvalho's—"

I corrected Claude sarcastically. "Gabriela. She wants to be called Gabriela."

The fat man continued. "Thank you, Englishman. I've spoken to Gabriela's assistant." Calling me Englishman—an attempt to bait me, a Scotsman, and not Claude's first attempt to bait me today—told me Claude's concern was limited. He had indulged me, but now we were on to business.

"Beatriz?" I asked. "You've spoken to Beatriz."

"If that's her name, then yes, I've spoken to her. I guess Miss Carv...Gabriela has several assistants."

"From what I saw, there's one assistant who pretty much runs everything, and then there are a number of other people to fetch and carry. And a security guy who may or may not be running his own show."

Claude winced but didn't argue. Instead, he took a sip of coffee. When he began to speak, his tone and the delivery had the quality I'd expect from a parent talking to a child when the parent knows they're in the moral wrong but still wants the kid to go along. It was in parts condescending, mollifying, and explanatory. He was also slightly exasperated. "Look. Gabriela is about to talk at some big conference at Le Palais des Congrès."

I knew of the venue. When Claude said big, he meant a conference with thousands of people. He also meant it to signal that it was something bigger than me. Something with which I couldn't argue.

"She's the main speaker. There are all sorts of protestors—"

"Protesting about?"

Claude half smiled. "Her. I told you, if you look at her from a business perspective, she's an angel; the CEO of one of Brazil's largest companies. If you're an environmentalist, she's the devil. Mining companies—especially mining companies that tear up the Amazon rainforest—are not good neighbors. The polar bear brigade is protesting outside the conference."

He leaned back in his chair and felt in his pocket, pulling out his cigars. He held up the pack as if to communicate that his need for a smoke had ended our conversation. He went to stand. "Sit. We're not done."

Claude placed his cigars on the table and sighed. "With the best will in the world, you can't see Gabriela. This woman—Beatriz? Did you say that was her name?—will call and arrange a time for you to talk. Probably tomorrow. Maybe later."

Claude was inventing the story as he went along.

"They'll call me; I'll call you if you give me your new number."

I felt my throat tightening. "There's a kid."

Claude made sure his pause and his considered nod communicated that he understood the point I was making beyond my words.

"Who's looking out for the kid? Has anyone told Gabriela that the exchange went to hell?"

Claude went to explain.

I stood. "I'm going to see her. I'll be there when she steps off the stage after making her speech. Call Beatriz and tell her to find a way to get me into the venue."

eight

I walked out from the warm cocoon of stale air that still embraced Claude.

My senses were assaulted—cold; damp air; the noise of angry traffic; streetlights, shop illuminations, and car headlights blinding. It wasn't past sunset, but it felt like the evening. As I lost my visibility, merging into the morass of people moving urgently in the chill and keen to reach their destination before the rain started again, I became aware of one dominant sound.

It was the sound of an engine—a big engine, diesel—being driven hard. There was a squeal of tires and a small skid. I looked around to see another knot of people discomforted by the aggression of the driving as a vehicle bumped up onto the curb.

A vehicle.

A black Land Cruiser.

I stepped out of the flow of pedestrians, into the shelter offered by a closed store frontage, and looked back. The driver got out of the vehicle, oblivious to the anxiety he had caused the pedestrians and not caring as he crossed their paths. The familiar suited figure disappeared into the café I had just left before his passenger had fully closed his door.

The passenger with his scruffy leather jacket was equally familiar. He took more care to avoid the pedestrians as he ran behind his master like a weak child struggling to walk as fast as his parent.

I counted to ten, making sure no one else emerged from the Land Cruiser, then slowly moved toward the café, inching forward to keep cover as I looked through the window.

The suited man was sitting across from Claude; the scruff was standing with a pose that was intended to look menacing, but that made him look like he had a stomachache. Claude was sitting bolt upright, the folds of fat in his face pulled tight. He didn't move; he just sat and observed as the better-dressed man spoke, his right hand had a rhythm motion that didn't seem to connect with the emphatic nods he was making.

The scruff moved first—he shifted before his boss had stopped talking. At first I thought he was headed to the bathroom, but then the suited man stood. I had a moment of panic, not able to decide whether to go up the street or down. I decided to go away from the direction the Land Cruiser was pointing to minimize the chances of being seen.

The man in the suit exited and crossed the pedestrian traffic as if there was no one there. He was pulling off as the scruff—who treated the pedestrians with marginally more respect and so took a few seconds longer to cross the strip of paving—reached his door.

Claude was still sitting bolt upright, his fat face pulled taut, when I reached him. I sat where the suited man had sat. The fat man was breathing, but it was like being in a room with a coma patient.

"What have you done? What have you got yourself into, Leathan?" I didn't see Claude's mouth move, but I heard the words. It felt more like my conscience talking to me than the man across the table from me.

We both fell silent.

"What have *I* done?" Claude had asked me a question, and only now the stupidity of what he asked struck me. "Me? What have I got myself into?" I sighed, long and loud. "You sent me."

Claude still seemed paralyzed from the neck up, but his hand was fumbling his jacket pocket. He pulled out a wallet, old and battered leather, like its owner. He grabbed all of his cash—I saw a €200, a €100, and several €50s, but there was more—and dropped it in front of me. "Go to the station, get on a train, and leave."

"What are you talking about, Claude? And who were those guys?"

"If you won't save yourself, at least do it for me. Don't make me a liar—don't let them find you here when I told them you freaked and decided to spend two weeks on the beach in Cape Town."

"Cape Town?"

"It was the first thing..." Claude shook himself, and his eyes locked on mine. "Just go, Leathan. I don't know what you've got yourself into, but there's no way that this story ends well for you or for me." His tone modulated. "You said there was shooting."

"Yeah, their third guy got hit."

"He's dead," said Claude. "He's dead and you're responsible, plus you owe them two million euros, not fake cash, so just go."

A silence fell between us again, and Claude sipped the dregs of his coffee, which was bound to be cold by now.

"You knew the guy," I said tentatively.

"Knew him, no. Recognized him, barely. Understood the weight he carries, certainly." Claude indicated to the waiter for another coffee. There were more hand gestures, which I presumed were Claude ordering food, and if he was eating, he was getting over his shock. "These are not the people I do business with or for, you must understand."

"Who?"

"That was Sylvain Mercier. He works for Augustin Guérin. They specialize in muscle, protection, extortion... you know the sort of thing."

"Kidnap?"

"Not that I've heard," said Claude. "Kidnapping requires patience, logistics—you've got to look after the hostage, move them around; it's high risk and slow. You need locations and patient people. Augustin Guérin has made his money by having men who don't mind throwing a fist for cash. He's never cultivated cautious people."

Claude's coffee arrived with a plate of something that was a combination of pastry and stickiness. "Monsieur?" said the waitress to me.

"No thank you," I said. "I'm about to leave."

"Where are you going to go?" asked Claude as the waitress departed.

"Exactly where I was going five minutes ago—to the conference center. And you're going to call Beatriz and make sure I can get in."

"This is a bad idea, Englishman," said Claude.

I was learning that when he called me Englishman, Claude was agitated. But his hope that calling a Scot English would rile me was wasted, and I ignored his attempt. "You're getting overexcited, Claude. Think about it—this Sylvain Mercier came to you. Why would he go to you if I'm their problem? How did he know to find you here—you're only here because it's been raining."

Claude closed his eyes as if acknowledging my implication was correct, even if he didn't want me to be right.

"If I'm right, there's someone on the inside. And if I'm right about that, then the kid's at much greater risk than Gabriela Carvalho realizes. Make the call to Beatriz."

I stood and left.

nine

It wasn't yet 4 PM, but under the thick blanket of raincloud on this early winter afternoon, it felt like night.

Claude was right, there were protestors outside the conference center. Where Claude had been mistaken had been on the scale of the protests, although by looking at the preparations, I suspected many more people had been expected.

The conference center, le Palais des Congrès, was an imposing concrete block set back from the road in the way that an imposing building should be. The conference center wasn't so much on a road, but technically, it was on a round-about. A huge roundabout where the police had parked their vans around the center before diverting both lanes of traffic to the other side of the circle.

In front of the conference center—and spilling onto the blacktop around the roundabout—were crash barriers to hold in the protestors. I counted; there might have been forty-five people expressing their view in this very public manner. If I was being generous, there were fifty people. Certainly not one hundred and definitely not a thousand. All were wet and bedraggled, and had little appetite but to stand and hold banners, most of which seemed homemade. They were the politest protestors I had seen since I had been in Paris.

The police—and I counted more than one hundred—seemed to concur with my general assessment that the protestors were not a threat. Most of the officers were sitting in their vans, chatting. A few in full riot gear—helmets; shields; arm, leg, and chest protectors—stood at the corners of the pen holding the protestors. One officer, probably more senior and wearing waterproof gear, stood to the side and observed.

One of the protestors began to chant. A second joined in. I felt a chilled gust come up from la Seine and drown out the sound. By the time the gust had passed, so had the desire by the protestors to chant.

"I'm here. Where do I go?" I asked Claude when he answered.

"Back entrance; they're expecting you."

"How do I get to the back entrance?" I asked as I watched the waterproofed policeman begin to slowly walk back to the vans.

"Can you see the front of the conference center?"

I stared up at the concrete structure that loomed above me. "Yeah. You can't miss it."

"Well, the back is on the other side. It's basic anatomy, Englishman. Go there. Find an entrance. They'll be waiting for you."

"Left or right?" I asked.

Claude had already hung up.

I flipped a coin in my head and went left, crossing the front of the conference center and looking at the protestors. I looked at each one in turn, wondering whether one of them could be responsible for Guilherme's disappearance. It made some sense to me on a day when little else made any sense.

As I rounded the corner, I was fairly sure where the entrance I was looking for was located. My guess was it would be somewhere close to where the dark Land Cruiser was parked and the two guys were chatting. Two guys who looked like the suited man I now knew as Sylvain Mercier and Gabriela Carvalho's driver Pierre Alvaréz. I couldn't be certain it was those two and I felt no compulsion to find out, so I spun and headed in the other direction.

I could wait until the Land Cruiser had gone.

ten

Across the road I found a place that gave me some cover. It gave better cover than it gave access to view the Land Cruiser. I figured that on balance it was preferable to be unseen while remaining uncertain about the identities. The alternative was to be certain—and I didn't want to be certain that Sylvain Mercier was pointing a gun at me. Again. I'd ignored Claude's advice, but I hadn't forgotten his warnings.

The conversation didn't last long—probably less time than it took to smoke a cigarette—and the Land Cruiser drove off at what passes for speed when you're moving a heavy lump of metal in the late afternoon Paris traffic.

The other guy—who looked like Gabriela's driver, Pierre Alvaréz—was gone. I jogged to where the conversation had taken place and found a side door to the conference center, which opened into a white foyer. It was sparsely furnished with a single sofa pushed back against a side wall. The main feature was the security guard sitting behind a desk facing the door. He stood; a giant—six ten, maybe more—wide, muscular, and with dark skin.

"Hi," I tried not to sound intimidated by the presence. "Leathan Wilkey. You should be expecting me."

The guard half-laughed, half-spoke, his voice a deep boom. "I was wondering how you pronounce that." He lifted a clipboard off his desk and pointed to the top sheet of paper. The pointing seemed more for his benefit than mine. He didn't offer anything more.

"So where am I going?"

He pointed to the only internal door.

With the outside of the building having been fashioned from concrete, I suppose I shouldn't have been surprised that the inside featured large quantities of concrete. The corridor was long, not particularly wide, and featureless.

I jogged, soon seeing someone in front of me, slowing to a walking pace as I caught him up. "Hi."

Pierre Alvaréz seemed shocked to see me. He stopped, half turning in the direction from which we had both come. His mouth moved, but it took a moment or two before sound started coming out. "You shouldn't be here...you should be... you need to leave now..." He spoke in French. It was clear he was not raised in France, but to my ear his grasp of the language was good and his accent was near perfect.

He placed his hands on my shoulders, trying to turn me. It wasn't an overtly aggressive gesture, more how you might physically point a child in the direction they need to walk. "You need to go now."

The comparison with Matheus Santos—heck, the comparison with me—was stark. There was something delicate about this man. When I first saw him across the reception room in the hotel suite, he looked like another member of Gabriela Carvalho's entourage that she had brought with her from Brazil. On the surface, he had appeared similar to Santos—dark business suit, white shirt, black hair cut short, and slightly olive skin. But up close he was different.

The hair was well cut. This was cut for style, not simply for function. His skin was clear—I suspected he had his own cleansing ritual and carried a small suitcase of unguents with him from Brazil. His hands were small and showed no callouses or cuts, and his nails had been perfectly manicured, giving just the right amount of white tip. Tips that were natural perfect crescents.

He might be trying to physically push me toward the door, but his personal presentation and his obvious lack of strength coupled with an inability to deploy what limited strength he did have told me that he was not the second man with Matheus Santos in the woods earlier this afternoon.

"But your friend might still be out there." I regretted the comment immediately—there was no need for him to know I had made the link to Sylvain Mercier.

The momentary flash across Pierre's eyes told me I was right to regret. "The guy I talked with outside?" he asked. His voice was so unemotional he could have been asking whether it was still raining. "The black Land Cruiser?"

I said nothing and tried to show no reaction.

"I went out for a smoke; he stopped to ask for directions." He paused. "They're looking for Versailles...but I think it's a bit late now. I suggested they go tomorrow."

I mumbled something, hoping he figured I believed his lie, then more clearly, "I need to see Gabriela. She's expecting me."

The driver shrugged and started walking. "You'd better follow me then."

eleven

We walked in silence. The driver seemed to know how to navigate through the maze of concrete corridors and passages.

Finally he led through a set of double doors, and there was a shift. The passage became wider, and the wall changed from concrete gray to render painted white; there was a ceiling concealing the pipes and cables, and a thin carpet on the floor. The temperature also changed, becoming warm enough that—in this place with no natural light, not that there was much daylight to be had outside—you might forget that it was cold and nearly night outside.

There were signs, lots of signs. Apart from the restroom signs, I wasn't sure where they might be directing—at a guess, the various conference rooms—and Pierre Alvaréz didn't seem ready to offer an explanation. Or indeed to communicate with me in any direct manner. He turned left through another set of double doors, which opened onto a room that was intended to offer more comfort—the carpet was thicker, the walls were a shade of beige, the ceiling was lower, and the lighting was warmer and less intrusive. There were several tables against the far wall, one with coffee jugs and clean cups stacked, another with an array of pastries. At various points around the room, there were low sofas—all of the same corporate complexion covered in burgundy fabric—with low side tables.

There were maybe fifteen people in the room, but it didn't feel crowded. I scanned. The first face I recognized was Beatriz Marques, her phone tight against her ear. She met my eyes and with her free hand she motioned for me to sit on the sofa closest to me. This wasn't a suggestion—it was a command in the same way that one might command a dog. Although I suspected a dog might pay less attention if its mistress spent her whole time talking on the phone.

There was little to gain by arguing, so I sat. The sofa offered the kind of comfort that I expected—in short, little comfort. It would be fine for five or maybe ten minutes, but it wasn't the sort of thing you would slob out on if you wanted to spend the night in front of the TV. The padding was minimal, and the back was too low to give any real support. But I didn't want to be here for any time, and any discomfort would keep me alert.

I continued to scan the room. Matheus Santos saw me before I saw him, but I had been distracted by the woman he was with. I hadn't seen her, or even a photo of her, but it was clear that this woman was in charge. Some things you just know immediately; then you look for evidence to confirm you aren't making the same mistake twice in one day.

There were some obvious traits—the woman had better-cut clothes than anyone else in the room. She wore a green dress—the green of the Brazilian flag—which was clearly tailored to her figure, not exaggerating or flattering. And then there was the gold. Gold earrings, a chunky gold necklace that a rapper might covet, two gold rings—one on each hand—and a number of gold bracelets and bangles.

I suppose the gold made sense for the chief executive of the company that was the largest miner of gold in Brazil.

But I was struck by how other people reacted to her. Santos was deferential; his body language suggested he would willingly throw himself on the floor should she not find the carpet to her taste—if she was chilly, then he would happily set himself on fire to provide some warmth. Beatriz, the assistant, was constantly looking, checking. A coiled spring ready for that slightest move that indicated she needed to rush in. And with each glance toward her boss, Beatriz exchanged a look with Santos, some sort of unspoken conversation going on between the two without the inclusion of their boss.

Then there were the other people in the room—I guessed journalists, conference organizers, maybe other speakers—all trying to be casual and not stare, but who had a look of unbridled excitement as they flicked glances toward the Brazilian wearing gold and green.

The only people who didn't seem to care about her were the conference center staff. Young people dressed in a familiar uniform of a white shirt with a vest on top, and a prominent name badge.

There was movement. Like a professional athlete making a pass—the ball was thrown not to the player, but to where the player was going to be. Beatriz Marques was moving next to Gabriela—and still talking on the phone that hadn't left her ear—while Matheus Santos was coming toward me.

For the few moments that I'd seen Gabriela Carvalho's security man walking in the hotel suite this morning, I hadn't noticed a limp. And from the way Santos seemed unused to the pain that was causing the reaction, I guessed it was new to him, too.

He sat on the same sofa as me awkwardly, not knowing how to hold his leg to minimize his discomfort. "Why are you here, Leathan?"

"Did you do that this morning?" I asked, pointing to the leg that was causing him discomfort.

"Slipped in the bathroom," he said with little conviction.

"Did you slip before or after you came to join us in Bois de Boulogne?"

He said nothing, his right hand beginning to massage his thigh.

"You were there," I continued. Still no reaction. "The kid wasn't."

Matheus Santos exhaled heavily, raised his eyebrows briefly, but offered nothing.

"They didn't seem like kidnappers to me," I offered. "More like three criminals who intended to steal the money."

Still no reaction.

"Not that you actually sent me with any money—just some shit you'd run off on a laser printer."

The security operative sighed heavily and fixed his gaze on me as he leaned forward. "Go home, Leathan. Your work's done. I'll make sure your fee gets forwarded to you by...what's his name? Claude, is that it?"

"Claude," I mouthed, breaking his eye contact and scanning the room again. Beatriz had ended her call and was talking with Gabriela. The senior woman concentrated absolutely on what the junior woman was saying.

"Go home, Leathan. I can organize a car."

"Is the kid...is Guilherme back?" I asked, turning my focus back to Matheus Santos.

Santos said nothing. His hand on his thigh was still, but his face lost some tone.

"Fuck up, conspiracy, or incompetence?" I asked. Santos frowned. "This morning. What went wrong and whose idea was it?"

"You'll get paid," said the security man.

"Does anyone actually care about Guilherme?" I asked.

"That's not your concern. You'll get paid."

"Who took him? What demands did they make?" There was a movement. Gabriela and her assistant had stopped talking, and Gabriela was heading toward the door through which I had entered with the driver. "I want to talk to her."

Santos' arm shot out. He held his hand over, but not touching, my chest, as if he had a personal force field that would keep me seated. "Your job is over. You'll get paid. And you can't speak to her; she's about to make her speech."

Gabriela left the room.

"Would you like me to organize a driver?" Santos relaxed his hand.

"The speech was hours ago," I said.

"They're running late. And now..." He snapped his fingers—not so much making a sound, but the gesture was intended to impress—and a smaller, younger version of him arrived. "This is Henrique." He turned to the younger man. "Henrique, this is Leathan; he's leaving. Make sure he doesn't get lost on his way out."

twelve

"Have you been working with Gabriela and Matheus for a long time?" I posed the question in French.

My handler—that was clearly young Henrique's intended function—recognized some of the words. "Gabriela" and "Matheus" in particular, I guessed. But whether he recognized any more, I wasn't sure.

"Yes, Gabriela and Matheus," he said. Four words, two of which were names. The other two were pretty common words—the kind you learn on day one when you're learning a new language and then use every day that you speak that new language. Of those two words, he badly pronounced one in French "oui," and said the other in Portuguese "e," and even then he lacked confidence.

"Is it better if I speak in English?" I said, trying to find a language in which we could converse.

"I speak little English." Four words, heavily accented, but all in English.

"Have you been working with Gabriela and Matheus for a long time?" I posed the question again, this time in English, speaking slowly.

We were in the main corridor with its thin carpet and white walls, heading in the direction from which I had arrived. "Yes," said my escort as we passed the restrooms.

"How long?"

Henrique held his hands, opening one finger at a time. I might have sneered if it weren't for the fact that I still count on my fingers when I talk in French. I looked at his hands and remembered the hands of the driver, Pierre. The driver's hands were small, delicate, manicured, moisturized, and cared for. My escort's hands, by contrast and despite his smaller frame, were huge lumps of meat, scarred and calloused, and with several very recent cuts.

If you told me he'd been in a scrap in Bois de Boulogne about three hours ago, I'd have believed you.

We headed through the double doors at the end and turned into the service corridor. The change from white walls and thin carpet to gray concrete décor demarcated the change from public to private. I stopped walking, turning back. "I need to use the bathroom."

Henrique shook his head. "No time," he said, waving me forward with one of the large lumps of meat protruding from the end of his sleeves.

"No, now," I said, gripping my stomach and wincing. I started to walk back toward the restrooms, taking small steps as if a longer step might lead to an accident.

Henrique sighed. "There's one up here," he said. "Come."

I turned and followed. He led me exactly along the path I had followed when I walked with Pierre Alvaréz. About fifty yards before we reached the white reception area with the large black security guard he stopped, gesturing to a door. "Here."

I hadn't noticed it when I arrived, but the sign said it was a restroom. I released a hand from my stomach and offered it to Henrique. "Thank you." More by reaction than desire he accepted my shake that I rapidly withdrew. "I need to hurry, but I'll see myself out—it's just there."

Henrique mumbled something as I turned and entered the small room. The door groaned behind me; I stopped, counted to ten—slowly and silently—and then opened the door, cautious to avoid any sound. When I stepped out of the bathroom, there was no sign of Henrique. I released the door and moved fully into the corridor, now unconcerned by the noise it was making.

I followed along the passage we had walked, walking as fast as I felt I could without drawing suspicion and without catching Henrique. But there was no sign of the young security operative with the rough hands. I paused before slipping through the double doors into the white corridor, looking for any sign of anyone who would recognize me, and then moved quickly, ducking into the ladies' restroom.

While impersonal, the room was surprisingly large. There were three stalls, discreetly shielded from the main area of the room where three sinks were set in an amply large faux marble surface, each sink having its own mirror edged with lights. The faucets were faux turn of the century—turn of the *last* century, and faux because these faucets were new and shiny and didn't leak.

One door in the three stalls was shut. Behind it was the quiet sound of someone moving. Heels gently clipping, clothes being smoothed, and then there was the soft rush of water. The lock on the door released, and there was a high squeal as the hinges moved.

The dark green dress and heavy gold jewelry told me I had guessed correctly where Gabriela Carvalho had been heading. She met my gaze, raised her eyebrows, then looked toward the sinks.

"I'm Leathan Wilkey," I said. "You hired me to make the exchange for Guilherme this morning."

"You need to speak to Matheus. I'll get him," she said, turning toward the exit.

I took two quick steps and blocked the door. She turned away and headed to the sink on the right, turning on the water and starting to wash her hands.

"We need to talk," I said.

"I'm already running late—if you hadn't noticed, my speech is already two hours overdue," she said, "and if you did some work for Matheus, then I can assure you that you will be paid in full."

"It's Matheus we need to talk about."

She turned off the faucet and picked a small towel to dry her hands, while slowly turning to me. Our eyes met, then she turned back, continuing to pat her hands dry.

"I was sent with fake cash," I said. "Think about it—fake cash for your kid's life. Then Matheus, and I'm guessing Henrique, jumped in waving guns and shooting."

I looked at her reaction in the mirror. I couldn't be sure what she was thinking, but this level of detail of what happened seemed new to her. "Don't worry—Guilherme wasn't there, so the shooting didn't affect him. Or do worry, Guilherme wasn't there, but Matheus didn't know that when he got his gun out and started shooting. And do worry, because no one seems to be taking this seriously."

Gabriela Carvalho was applying lipstick as she spoke. "I can assure you, Lee...I'm sorry, I don't know how to pronounce your name correctly. But I can assure you that I take my son's welfare very seriously and so does Matheus Santos. We will both make sure whoever is responsible for this pays." She finished her lipstick and continued. "And now I've got a speech to make."

"Police," I said. "You need the police. You need to stop Guilherme being taken out of the country."

She turned and headed toward me, waiting for me to step aside. I did. She paused, looking expectantly from me to the door and back. It took me a moment, but I got the hint and opened the door for her.

thirteen

I let the door swing closed. I couldn't follow Gabriela Carvalho—she would attract attention, and Matheus Santos would realize I hadn't left, assuming he didn't find out the moment Gabriela complained to him about my intervention.

The door started to move, slowly and then more quickly. I stepped back as a woman I didn't recognize entered. "Oh." There was shock in her voice. She turned as if to leave.

"No need to worry, madame," I said. "Undercover security... You've seen the protestors outside. I just needed to check and I'm leaving now. Everything's safe—there are no bombs here."

My last comment seemed to introduce an element of terror that she had not contemplated. I left before she could question me and walked toward the room where I had first seen Gabriela Carvalho, slipping through the door and trying to find some camouflage with the small gatherings in the room.

"What are you still doing here?" There was annoyance in Beatriz Marques' tone—but not enough annoyance to pry the phone from her ear. "And you upset Gabriela..." She seemed about to say more, but her conversation distracted her and she placed her other hand to the right of my chest, nearly at my shoulder, indicating I should remain still.

As she hung up I said, "They haven't told you, have they?" She made the smallest movement of her head. "Matheus sent me with fake cash, and then he and Henrique tried to snatch the kid."

There was a beat—a moment—where this highly efficient organizing machine tried process the new data it had received. One new piece of information bumped up against an old piece, and there was conflict. Conflict in her brain and hesitation. Two processing algorithms and no way to resolve which took precedence—did she rely on the fact she knew to be true, or was this new piece of information more important? Did this new possibility throw the veracity of her knowledge into question?

"I'm just trying to do the right thing for the kid," I said. "No one else seems to care about him." The efficient machine was ready to rebut my criticism, but I continued. "Matheus is about faking and fighting, Gabriela seems to be more worried about the affront to her, and you seem to be more concerned about keeping the show on the road."

I had criticized three people, including her, personally. Beatriz was deciding which criticism to rebut first, but something was still niggling with her. Something I had said had resonated.

"I'm just trying to find Guilherme and to make sure he's safe." I made the statement again, hoping to clarify my intent before I moved forward. "You know something's not right."

She didn't try to argue. She didn't try to hide that her silence implied a certain agreement.

"Who don't you trust?" I asked. "Around Gabriela...who don't you trust?"

She leaned forward as if she were going to say something, then stopped.

"Okay. Who don't you like?"

A small grin came across her lips, but no words slipped out.

I mirrored the grin. "I need a chat—a proper, sensible chat—with Gabriela. When is she free?"

Beatriz seemed almost relieved with a question she could answer. "She's just started speaking, so it'll be at least ninety minutes." Pierre Alvaréz walked across my line of sight, heading to the coffee table.

"When will you be back at the hotel?"

She muttered about meeting and eating, then said, "Eight."

"Okay, I'll…" I let the sentence hang—she could interpret it how she wanted. "I need to be off."

Beatriz seemed relieved that her interrogation was over. Her brain clicked onto the next item on her mental checklist. "Guilherme? Matheus said…" It was her turn to leave details unsaid. I shrugged and turned away, heading to the coffee table and the pastries beyond.

"Hi," I said to Pierre, the driver and my first escort, as I positioned him between me and the table of pastries. "I'm just going for…and I'll be off." I pointed over his head as if he were a large object in the path to my destination.

He stepped left as if to let me pass. I went left. He stepped right—half smiling at our mild confusion. I went right and stepped forward knocking into him gently. "I'm sorry, Pierre; that was my fault completely."

fourteen

In my left hand I held two sticky pastries and in the right Pierre Alvaréz's phone. I knew the route out—this was my fourth time following this concrete path through the conference center.

Pierre might be fluent in many languages, he might have perfect skin and delicate hands, but he wasn't smart when it came to phones. He wasn't smart in letting me remove it from his pocket as I walked into him, apparently accidentally, and he wasn't smart in not adding a passcode. And no passcode meant I could check his call log.

Where he was smart—or maybe lazy—was in not using the address book. All I had were numbers, no names. I took a bite from my pastries with the grace of a caveman chewing off a lump of meat and hit redial to call the last number Pierre had called. A number he had called maybe five minutes earlier today.

"Pierre." The accent was Brazilian—a Brazilian talking with someone she was familiar with. The voice was high and squeaky. It was familiar, but it took a few moments to recognize who was speaking. Even though I hadn't seen her, I recognized the voice of Luiza, Guilherme's nanny who had been so upset this morning.

It's hard to gauge how upset someone is from one word—a name—spoken maybe seven or eight hours after the event that caused the upset, but she didn't seem that upset now.

I hung up then tried the next few numbers—all local Paris numbers—and rapidly came to the conclusion that Pierre was a big fan of the female of the species. That said, one sounded older and at a guess was his mother. A French mother might explain the driver's grasp of the language— my French mother had ensured I was fluent in both of my parents' native languages—and Pierre's French forename with a possibly Portuguese/Brazilian surname made some sort of sense.

I flicked back to earlier in the day. There was a burst of calls between 9 AM and 10 AM to five numbers. I tried them all as I walked. All of the numbers—numbers where this morning Pierre had undertaken calls lasting several minutes—now rang without answering.

I stuffed the remainder of the pastries into my mouth and took out my phone to photograph the call logs.

The big black security guard was still on duty. "I found this phone just back there," I said, placing Pierre Alvaréz's phone on the desk in front of him. "Can you find an owner?"

"Sure," he said, looking up from his clipboard where he was writing the time against my name.

fifteen

I stepped from the functional white lobby into the noise of the street slightly dulled by the light rain, and let the cool early evening air fill my lungs. Turning left, I headed toward the front of the building and its main entrance, where the protestors and the riot police had congregated.

He stepped out from the shadows—similar shadows to those in which I had hidden earlier while watching him. Then I felt something in my back—hard, metal—someone holding something on me.

"Hi," I said, smiling broadly, keeping my speech bright.

Sylvain Mercier half smiled and raised his eyebrows. I wasn't sure if he was amused by my reaction or surprised at how simple it had been to find me and apprehend me.

And I wasn't sure how I could be caught so easily. Since I'd decided to stay in Paris I had taken precautions to ensure that the reason I was no longer living in London—a Bulgarian human trafficking gang—didn't find me. If two local criminals could locate me so easily, then it wouldn't be difficult for the Bulgarians to find me. And it wasn't as if I didn't have the option to do something like leave by a different door. But then again, I didn't expect the Bulgarians to turn up when there were so many cops just around the corner.

I was pushed from behind. A quick flick of my head before I returned to concentrate on the direction in which I was being pushed confirmed it was the guy with the scruffy leather jacket who held a gun on me this morning. And if not the one who held the gun, it was the friend of the one who held the gun. Whichever one he was, in evolutionary terms this guy was the fittest—he had survived. His friend hadn't—he had died after receiving a bullet in his gut. If this guy was the survivor, then I figured my chances of making a lucky break twice in a few hours were low.

I was jostled again, and Sylvain Mercier indicated I should follow, half turning as he began to walk in the direction I was being pushed. I let my eyes scan the row of parked cars. A short way down one stood out—larger than the others. A black Land Cruiser.

I was pushed into the backseat, and the guy with the gun followed.

Sylvain Mercier got into the driver's seat before firing up the engine. We pulled into the traffic and then Mercier hit the pedal hard, coaxing a satisfying rumble from the large diesel engine as we moved with little finesse.

The Land Cruiser pulled onto a more substantial road with traffic flowing. Mercier leaned to reach, then tossed something back. "Put it on."

The guy with the gun caught it and in a single flowing move took the lump of fabric, which had the appearance of a small bag but was doubtless intended as a hood, and gripped either side, his gun sitting uneasily in his right hand. "Your head," he said.

As my world changed from one of electric light to one of dark, I reflected that the last call Pierre Alvaréz made was to Luiza the nanny, not to a number that might be linked to these guys.

sixteen

We drove for about half an hour. My main conclusion from the drive was that Sylvain Mercier didn't have a future as a chauffeur—he lacked both skill and temperament.

The Land Cruiser stopped and the engine was killed. The driver's door opened, and Mercier exited the car. I sat in near silence with the scruffy guy. With my hood still firmly in place, I knew he was there by his uneven breathing—it was like he was forcing air through a tube that was too narrow—and by the squeak of his jacket as he twitched.

My door came open, and I was led up three flights of stairs before being pushed into a wooden chair. I felt the zip ties tighten to hold my wrists against the chair, and my hood was tugged off to reveal a small room. A living room in need of decoration and maybe a move from the 1950s to perhaps the 1990s if the twenty-first century was too much of a stretch.

Sylvain Mercier pulled up a chair, heavy and wooden with some padding on the seat. It looked much like the chair I felt I was tied to. "Where's my money?"

"Probably wherever you left it," I tried. "Untie me and I'll help you look."

There was the squeak of leather to my right. Mercier looked in the direction of the squeak and gave more of a shake of his eyes rather than a shake of his head.

"Thank you," he said, turning his focus back to me. "That's a very kind offer, but I don't think I was clear. Where are my two million euros that you took?"

There was a groan of leather to my right as the twitchy scruff moved. "Could someone find a seat for..." I turned my head to face him. "I'm sorry, I don't know your name."

"Jordan," he muttered.

"Could we get a seat for Jordan?" I asked, turning back to Mercier. Mercier's focus was on the other man, the man I now knew as Jordan. Mercier raised his eyebrows and then started moving his eyes toward my gaze.

There was a squeak of leather, and a fist landed in my gut. I felt the air leave my lungs in a sudden rush and a deep, low sound of pain come out of my mouth as I doubled over, instinctively pulling at my wrists to grab my stomach, but failing. The momentum of the chair rocking back stopped, and it began to tip forward until the legs hit the floor, vibrating to a halt.

"That's why Monsieur Roussel is standing," said Mercier as I tried to sit straighter. "Would you him like to explain in more detail?"

"No," I said weakly.

"Good," said my interrogator. "Now, you were about to tell me where you have stored my money."

"Stored?"

"I'm sure that's what you've done. You've stored my two million euros somewhere safe so that it didn't get lost. And I'm grateful for that, but now...now I'd like my money back. Just tell me where it is, and we can go and get it."

I calibrated. What could I say that would not lead to a fist in my gut? Or worse.

Mercier looked up to the other man. I saw one half of a conversation pass and then Jordan—Monsieur Roussel, as Mercier had referred to him—straightened and headed out of the room. There was low glow as a light went on in the next room, running water, and then the sound of an electric kettle being switched on. Roussel returned.

"Boiling water," said Mercier to no one in particular.

"They called me this morning," I said. Mercier feigned surprise that I was talking to him. "They wanted someone local—someone who spoke the language—to make the exchange."

Mercier defocused and cocked his head as if listening to a sound at a distance. From the next room—the kitchen,

I presumed—the sound of water beginning to boil in the electric kettle was unmistakable.

"I was just the guy who made the exchange. They gave me the bag—I didn't look inside. I didn't know it was meant to be two million euros. I didn't know it was fake currency." I could hear my pitch rising as my throat tightened. "Do you think if I had two million euros that I'd spend my time driving around Paris? Don't you think I'd be on a beach somewhere surrounded by girls in bikinis? Lots of girls...less with the bikinis."

I didn't know much about Mercier, but in my few interactions with him, I'd begun to form the opinion that he might not be much of a poker player. Not that I played—if I wanted to waste money, I'd rather waste it on a horse. But Mercier seemed incapable of controlling his reactions. His face was a mass of tells. It would take some time to figure what each tell told me, but for the moment I knew that my basic proposition—that if I had two million euros I'd have gotten the heck out of Paris—had resonated.

His gaze returned to me, but he said nothing. His breathing was regular but heavier, as if he needed to suck in more oxygen to power his brain.

I broke his contemplation. "And you don't have the kid."

He didn't say anything, but his look was one of outrage. He had the look of a dowager duchess in a BBC period drama who was about to exclaim: "How dare you!"

"Be outraged. Argue with me all you like, but you don't have the kid." I tried to keep the smile off my face, but I could feel the involuntary pull of the muscles at the side of my mouth. "Come on! Your demand gives it away."

There was the sound of Roussel shifting his weight. Mercier waved a hand, more like someone batting a fly than an instruction to the other man not to inflict pain, and frowned. An unspoken question.

"You asked for too much, but not enough."

The frown remained, but there was a slight twist of his head, encouraging me to elaborate.

"The kid is worth way more than two mill. The mother's loaded, there's her company, and there'll be insurance. But you chose a figure that you reckoned could be raised quickly. Any CEO who flies in on a private jet can quickly raise two million, right? But getting ten or twenty is probably harder."

Mercier's face had finally taken on the look of a poker player. No need for him to visit the Mona Lisa to learn about inscrutability.

"You learned that the kid had been taken, and before anyone made contact or the disappearance became public, you made a ransom demand and asked for what you figured was the most you could get." I paused, smiled, shook my head gently to ham up my show of slightly awed disbelief. "You kidnapped the kidnap. I love it! That was smart."

Mercier tried to hide his grin but failed. As he returned his stare to me, something changed in his face. It hardened. Maybe regret. Maybe he was realizing that I had twigged the plan—and if I could twig, then so could others.

"If you don't have a hostage, it's going to be difficult to demand a ransom for the second time."

Mercier went to disagree. I wasn't sure whether he was going to argue that he could still demand a ransom or if he was playing out another scenario in his head.

"You haven't learned much, have you?" He twitched, so I continued. "This is chess, and you started out so well, forcing them into action. But—if you'll excuse the change of sport—they played you, not the ball, and you didn't notice."

"But—" began Mercier.

"Look at how they're behaving." I cut across him. "They're not in a hurry. They know that whoever's got the kid won't harm him because a dead kid has no value."

He was breathing heavily again.

"That said, there's still money to be made."

A simple statement, but I had his attention again. He waited patiently, his head lolling forward as if he were encouraging me to elaborate, but then pulling himself back when he seemed too keen.

I said nothing.

Mercier's brow furrowed. I tried to guess which aspect he was looking at—the thought of money or the notion of telling his boss there was a problem, assuming Augustin Guérin didn't already know what was happening, and with the death of the third man earlier today, I suspected he did.

"You may not have the kid," I said. "But there'll be a finder's fee."

He tried to play it cool. He tried to behave as if his brain wasn't reacting like a kid who had been offered all the candy he could eat. He might not know how much it was, but he'd clearly already decided that however much a finder's fee was, it would be sufficient pay for a day's work when split two ways and with tribute paid to Augustin Guérin.

"You need some help," I said.

Mercier laughed loudly. "Are you offering to help? Think you might get a share of my money?"

"No," I said, knowing that my face was not communicating the anger the other man was now showing. "I'm not here to take your money—I just care about getting the kid home."

"And you want to help us?"

"Not especially. I was just going to suggest something that would help you."

"Is he for real?" asked the scruff Roussel, moving more clearly into my arc of sight. I'd forgotten about him and his boiling water.

"Hear me out," I began. A glance passed between the two, and they turned back to me. "If you hold onto me, I'm just dead weight—I can do nothing for you. To be sensible, you should just kill me, but of course there's the chance that you'd get caught for that."

"Nah," said Roussel, "we wouldn't."

I tried to ignore the threat, which sounded more like a statement of fact based on past experience. "But if you let me go, then I'm going to be searching for the kid. I'm not saying I'll find him, but I'll certainly shake things up, and whoever you've got on the inside of Gabriela Carvalho's entourage, they'll be able to tell you what I'm up to and what's going on."

"Why would they...?" began Roussel.

Mercier held up a hand to stop the other man, a flash of anger across his face. I took my chance to continue. "There's no point in keeping me: I'm no benefit and all risk. And outside this room I can't hurt you—I don't have an army."

Something amused Roussel.

"Think about it: If I get a lead, you've just got to get there before me."

seventeen

I didn't ask where I was being driven, and I didn't complain when they put the hood over me again; I was just pleased to have my wrists released. I was pleased to be out of the room and away from the boiling kettle.

After a while it became clear from the sounds and from the change in driving pattern that we were in heavier traffic. I relaxed, letting my eyelids shut. I opened them rapidly when I felt the hood being pulled off. We had pulled up, and I was pushed out of the Land Cruiser, which drove off.

It took me a few moments to recognize that I was at the junction of Champs-Élysées and Avenue George V, the road where Gabriela Carvalho's hotel stood. It was a short walk, and I reached the hotel at about 6 PM.

I wasn't sure whether anyone would be there, but I guessed one or more of Gabriela Carvalho's team would be around. I was surprised when Beatriz Marques opened the door, and she was clearly surprised to see me. Surprised, but I also picked up on what I took to be relief.

She was still on the phone and still talking, but with her free hand she invited me in, closing the door behind me. Then she hugged me with her free arm, holding me for momentarily longer than I expected.

She hung up and released me simultaneously. "Is Gabriela here?"

She nodded without looking at me—her gaze was fixed on her phone, which was held in one hand, her thumb dancing over the screen to type out a message. "She's running late—you need to be quick." The assistant led me through into the reception room with its many doors and its window onto the less attractive side of Paris, which now that it was illuminated had a certain beauty. "Gabriela," she called and then turned to the woman I hadn't met before who was sitting on sofa. "This is Luiza Pérez."

"Guilherme's nanny," I said before she could elaborate. I smiled my acknowledgement to the nanny—she nodded her response. "Matheus and Pierre not around?" I asked to no one in particular.

"Gone to get the car ready for Gabriela," said the nanny. Finally, I was able to connect the high-pitched voice I had heard to a body. In this case, a slim and featureless body albeit topped with a pretty face and shoulder-length straight hair.

I was distracted by a noise behind me. Footsteps and an intentional exasperated sigh. The green dress was now red, but the gold remained. The heavy, chunky gold had been replaced by something more delicate. "Why do you always turn up when I'm running late?"

"And it's good to see you again, Gabriela."

She smiled. A smile that had doubtless disarmed many men before. Behind me there was a shuffling, and Luiza Pérez moved off the sofa and left the room. It seemed that Beatriz had left us, too.

The chief executive stood in front of the window, looking at her reflection and adjusting her outfit. She smoothed, tucked, turned at different angles, all the time keeping her focus on her reflection.

I began. "You don't seem to be showing the concern I would expect for someone whose kid has just been kidnapped."

She stopped and turned to face me, her mouth slightly open. "How can you say that I do not love my son?"

"That's not what I said."

"I know very well what you said," she spat under her breath.

"So why aren't you doing something?"

"Like?" she asked.

I hesitated.

She laughed. At me. "Precisely. What is it that I'm not doing? Is your problem that I'm working?" She paused for half a beat—long enough to imply that I hadn't answered her question but not sufficient time to let me respond, and then continued. "Do you know how many thousands of people work for my company? Many very poor people whose only possible source of income for their whole family comes from employment with my company. Do you know what would happen to those people if I decided to..." she sighed heavily, "if I decided to do whatever it is you think I should be doing? And what is that? Sit in my room and weep?"

"I was just suggesting..." I tried.

"Suggesting what?" She fixed her stare on me. "You come here and criticize me—you tell me I'm not behaving like I should, but I don't see you holding Guilherme's hand, bringing him back to me. You tell me how I should behave, but I don't see you doing anything practical to help the situation."

I didn't know what to say. I had a lot I wanted to say, but I didn't know what to say first.

"In case it has escaped your notice, I have a team of people here in Paris—and there are more beyond those you've already met. And that team is working hard. In a situation like this it is important that we send out a message. If we don't send out a message, then this will just happen again. People need to know that if they try, they will fail, and the consequences of their failure will be catastrophic for them."

My voice was weak when I spoke. "What about Guilherme? Aren't you worried about his safety?"

"Of course I am!" She realized that she had raised her voice to an unnecessary level. "Of course I am, but I also know that whoever has got him will look after him. He's a source of money to them, and I can offer more money than they can ever imagine for Guilherme's safe return."

"So why don't you call the police—put the airports on alert. Call their resources."

She laughed. "I trust my team."

"But you don't know who you're dealing with here," I said. "There are at least two groups trying to get money—only one of them has Guilherme—and you've got a leak on the inside."

"On the inside of my team?" She didn't try to hide her skepticism.

"My money's on Pierre," I offered. "But I can't prove anything yet."

She snorted derisively. "Look, you've done your job, you'll get paid. But please don't tell me you know more about my son's welfare than I do."

There was a subtle cough. Beatriz was standing by the entrance. "Your car is here." She turned and the chief executive followed her, leaving me alone in the room.

eighteen

Luiza Pérez was sitting on a bed watching a music video on her phone. A thin white cable ran from her lap to her ears. She had the look of a surly teenager trying to avoid an interfering parent. Not the appearance of the adult who had been charged with the safety of a child when he had been snatched this morning.

The room was large. This wasn't some pokey box for the staff. There was a double bed on which she sat and a second single bed that had a children's book on the nightstand. A row of closets had a business suit on a hanger hooked over one of the doors. A business suit suitable for a seven-year-old.

Everyone handles stress in their own way. Everyone deals with crises in a way that gets them through. There are no rulebooks saying if bad thing A happens, then you are required to adopt upset behavior B.

Intellectually, I understood the principle, but that didn't stop me from having expectations, and no one seemed to be offering a reasonable reaction to Guilherme being snatched.

His mother seemed more concerned about keeping her business appointments and ensuring vengeance was wrought upon the perpetrator. Gabriela's security had been more concerned about playing the hero. The assistant, Beatriz, had been focused on her phone, although to be fair to her, she did seem to be starting to see my position.

And the nanny was watching music videos on her phone.

I sat on the bed. Some might suggest my positioning was aggressive, maybe intrusive. If they wanted to say that, I wouldn't disagree, that was rather the intention. I wanted to intimidate the young woman. I wanted her on edge. I wanted her to feel a twinge of fear...some apprehension.

The change in her breathing told me she had noticed me. The tightening of the muscles told me she was trying to pretend she hadn't noticed or was cool with me sitting on her bed. If she noticed, I could wait—it would just get more uncomfortable for her.

So I waited. The breathing remained labored and her position was like she had been fixed in stone. Eventually she pulled her earphones out. She didn't say anything, but there was an implied teenage sigh. I guess that in moving from being a teenager to being a young adult, she had learned to control her sighing.

But more subtly, through a small movement, she had flipped the initiative back to me. It was my turn to take a move.

"You got out of the room quickly when Gabriela came in," I started. "I thought you might have something to say about Guilherme's disappearance."

She shrugged but said nothing.

I tried a different approach. "You seem close with Pierre Alvaréz."

She wanted to shrug again, but there was confusion across her face. "Why shouldn't I be—he's the only one here who's any fun." It was that squeaky voice.

"Fun?"

"Do they have fun in your country?"

"I thought your job wasn't about fun, but to care for Guilherme."

"I'm thirty-one years old and spent four years to qualify as a nursery nurse. I know my job and I know how to care for a child—in fact, I'm quite good at it, certainly better than..." She let the thought hang. "I'm allowed to have fun, and Guilherme is allowed to have fun. I suppose you wouldn't understand that if you're enjoying yourself, it makes learning so much easier and so much more effective."

She didn't look thirty-one—she looked ten years younger than that, but I didn't doubt her. And I suspected her claim to be qualified would likely be true—it seemed implausible that Gabriela would not have vetted this woman extensively before she hired her. But she was the one who had spoken with Pierre Alvaréz, the man who I'd seen talking with Sylvain Mercier, and she was the one who had been with the kid when he was grabbed. Looked at that way, she was the first person not to call the police.

"You know your job," I began, "but Guilherme was snatched while he was with you." She looked away. "And are you really telling me that four years at college gives you better insight than a mother? Are you saying that four years at college means you love the kid more than a mother?"

She got angry faster than I expected, which was good because I was running out of ways to needle her. "You don't know anything!" she shouted. "I'm the only one who cares about Guilherme. The only one." Her breathing was heavy, as if she had just been running. "I'm the one who wants him to be a kid. To do what kids do, to play, to learn, to have fun, to draw, to mess about in the mud with other kids...."

Luiza stood and walked to the closet, then continued in her high-pitched tone. "She wants him to dress like a ridiculous mini-businessman in this stupid suit." She held the suit that was hanging on a closet door. "She wants to pretend like he's some executive in her business so that they can take photos."

The nanny flopped onto the single bed, dropping the tiny suit beside her. "You know the sad thing? Gabriela can only relate to the kid when he dresses like a businessman. Put him in shorts and a T-shirt and have him kick around the ball, and she doesn't get it. 'Mama, look how far I kicked the ball!' he'll shout at her—he'll be delighted—but she'll have lost interest. It's me who'll be there clapping and cheering. It's me who tells him he will play for Brazil in the soccer World Cup."

The room fell quiet, and Luiza Pérez began to get her breath back. I looked around—there was little of her in the room, but there was a lot that belonged to the kid. I guessed the soccer ball was his. The three pairs of shoes—sneakers, deck shoes, and black brogues to accompany the suit—would never fit her. Some playing cards, slightly larger than casino-standard cards. Books. Books to read. Books to color and coloring pencils.

I went to speak. Luiza stood, waving a finger. "No, don't say anything. Wait there."

She left the bedroom, walking swiftly, her stockinged feet hitting the carpet with sufficient impact to make a noise. There was rustling and something fell over, then she returned holding a magazine. I didn't recognize the publication, but I recognized the type: glossy, thick paper, lush photographs, aspirational stories crafted by PR professionals, and lots of advertising for high-end goods. "Look," she said, sitting on the bed next to me and showing me the cover.

Gabriela stared back at us. A single primary-color dress and gold jewelry.

Luiza flipped open the magazine and turned some pages until another image of Gabriela stared out—a different primary color and different gold jewels. The nanny checked to make sure my attention was focused on the magazine, then flipped the page. Another image of Gabriela. She was in sharp focus and the background was slightly blurred; however, it was clear that the photo had been shot in a corporate setting—there were the usual hallmarks, big windows overlooking over a city, a desk, a big chair, awards and trophies, and a framed photo on a desk.

The page turned again. "Look," said Luiza defiantly. The location was the same office, but Gabriela had been joined in the picture by a kid who I took to be Guilherme. Guilherme wearing the business suit that was now laying on his bed. Gabriela was leaning back on her desk. Her head was turned upwards, and the smile across her face was delightful. Her son stood on the desk next to her, his head higher than hers. His smile was the smile that kids make when they are told to smile for the camera.

"You seem more upset for yourself," I said. It was partly true, but I needed to push her some more. "You think Gabriela's a terrible mother, and you're showing me pictures that show she uses the kid as a prop, but you don't seem to be concerned that Guilherme has been taken and is being held hostage."

"He's safe," said Luiza under her breath and without thinking.

The room suddenly felt very quiet. Luiza was sitting next to me trying not to move, as if that would slow down time and once she had slowed it, she could stop it. And once time was stopped, then she could wind it back and unsay what had just fallen out of her mouth.

I slipped off the bed and dropped to my knees in front of the nanny, then moved away the magazine and took her hands in mine. "Where is he, Luiza? Where is Guilherme?"

She said nothing but started shaking her head.

"Luiza..."

Tears began to form at the side of her eyes.

"You know where he is." It was a statement, but also an implicit question.

She hesitated—not for long, but for long enough to tell me she knew something—and then shook her head.

"Okay," I said. "You don't know where he is, but you *suspect* you know where he is."

She didn't say anything, but she pulled back from me.

nineteen

The bellboy had tried to usher us back inside as he flagged a cab, but I wanted to be away from the prying eyes and the prying ears of the hotel's lobby. I also hoped the chill of the early evening might connect with Luiza on some emotional level and make her consider Guilherme's situation. The evening was cold, so maybe Guilherme was cold. She had no way of knowing for certain that he wasn't.

I stood close—I needed to make sure I could grab her if she ran—and leaned in to speak. "Where is he?"

"I don't know," she said. "I told you, I don't know where Guilherme is."

"So how can you be so sure he's safe?"

"I know."

"How? How do you know?" I waited. "How can you be sure he's being fed properly? And what if there's a problem—you know that sometimes kids just get sick. Really sick. Needs a hospital now sick. What happens then? How do you know he's safe?"

Luiza said nothing.

"You don't get it, do you?" I said. "We—you and me—are going to get Guilherme and bring him back here." I articulated each word clearly, pausing for her to take in the information and process the details. "We're going to find him, make sure he's safe, and bring him back. Once we know Guilherme is safe, then whether you hang around is entirely up to you—I'm just worried about the kid. If you want to bolt, that's fine by me; I wasn't hired to find you."

She looked up at me but still said nothing.

"We do have another option." Hope flickered in her eyes. I extinguished it quickly. "I haven't told Gabriela. I haven't told Matheus. I haven't told Beatriz. I haven't told anyone that you're involved, but as soon as I tell someone... Well, then it's the law of the jungle, and I don't know if you know how much Matheus Santos enjoys playing with guns and likes to do what Gabriela wants without thinking too hard or questioning. And make no mistake, Gabriela cares about retribution."

Luiza had a hand to her mouth, her thumbnail slipped between her two front teeth—a childlike action, but with an adult's control neither to suck her thumb nor to bite her nail. "I don't know where they've taken Guilherme." There was little conviction in her statement.

"You don't know, but you suspect."

Luiza hesitated, then dropped her thumb and went to her bag. It was a large bag, the main purpose of which seemed to be to carry supplies that may be needed by Guilherme: tissues, band-aid, wipes, a book, more tissues—this time an open pack spilling into the bag—pens and pencils, scraps of paper, her phone....

I reached in and grabbed her phone. "It would be a shame to ruin the surprise of our arrival."

Luiza continued looking through her bag, opening up scraps of paper, then pulled one out. "This is all I know," she said.

I grabbed the scrap. I didn't know the street, but I knew the suburb, Saint-Cloud. Quiet, residential, moneyed, and just outside the southwest edge of the city.

"Monsieur," said the bellboy, indicating the cab that was waiting. I slipped him a €50 bill—far too generous for calling a cab, but something told me I wanted him to remember us.

I pushed Luiza into the backseat and gave the cabbie the address as I followed her in.

As the cab pulled out, the nanny began to remonstrate with me. It wasn't so much a reasoned discourse, more a string of fragments. "It's not my fault." Or, "She's a bad mother." And "Guilherme would be better off without her." Then, "That company's bad for the environment—she's destroying the Amazon."

At some point I stopped listening.

twenty

The evening traffic moved slowly. Occasionally the cab driver flicked on the wipers, and from time to time he adjusted the heat to clear the condensation from inside the windows.

Luiza had fallen silent at about the time the cab crawled over the bridge taking us across la Seine. The quiet was a relief—I was bored listening to her justification about why she had let the kid be put in danger, even if she didn't see it as danger. But I needed her there. I needed her to look after the kid—if and when we found him—and I needed her there so she wouldn't tell anyone we were on our way. There were too many people she could tell, starting with whoever had the kid and moving on to Gabriela and Matheus.

The cab continued moving slowly, like the last drop of toothpaste being pushed out of a tube, and then we stopped. In front all I could see were red lights going away from us and white lights coming toward. To our rear, the same.

She was fast. The door opened, and she ran. Before I got across the seat and out of the cab, she had disappeared into the crowd of people lining the sidewalk. Commuters, office workers...people just wanting to get out of the cold and damp. There was no ripple. No hint as to where she might be.

I got back in the cab and shut the door. "What do you want me to do?" asked the driver.

"Drive."

He sighed. "Drive after her or drive where we were going?"

"Do you know where she went?" I asked.

"Where we were going then," said the driver, falling silent but unable to move in the traffic.

I pulled out Luiza's phone and started flicking through her call log. For the second time today, a phone without a password. Nothing jumped out at me, so I went to her contacts and found Beatriz.

"Luiza?" She answered on the first ring.

"No, it's Leathan."

"Oh." Gabriela's assistant quickly got over her surprise. "Is everything alright?"

"You mean apart from a kid being kidnapped?" I snarked and instantly regretted it. "Sorry. That was unnecessary."

She muttered something about it not mattering, but I suspected she was focused elsewhere and the snark hadn't really registered. "Are you still at dinner?" I asked.

"Yes," she said, more instinctively than because she had fully considered the question.

"Can you just pay attention for a moment?" I asked. "This is important."

"Sorry," she said.

"It's Luiza. Luiza is involved somehow. I don't know how, but she's involved."

"Are you sure?"

"Certain that she's involved," I said and recounted my conversation with the nanny and our journey until her departure.

"But might she just be uncomfortable with you?" said Beatriz. "Maybe she felt you forced her into the cab?"

"I kinda did," I said quietly. "That was the point."

"I need to talk with Luiza to clear this is up. Where did she go? What's she going to do now?" asked the assistant.

"I don't know, and that's why I'm telling you."

There was silence on the other end of the line. For the first time since I had met her, I was convinced that I had the assistant's full attention. When she spoke, it was slow and measured. "So what are you going to do now?"

"I'm going to look for Guilherme where Luiza thinks he is."

twenty-one

I asked the driver to drop me a street away.

I paid the fare, plus fifteen percent tip give or take, rounded up to the next bill. In short, I was generous but not overgenerous. Unlike the bellboy at the hotel, I didn't want this guy to remember me, although somehow I felt that if the cops asked him he would already remember this journey with clarity.

When I say I asked the driver to drop me on the next street, that implies I knew where I was actually going. And while it was true that I did have an address—the scrap of paper I had retrieved from Luiza Pérez before she bolted from the cab and found invisibility in a crowded Parisian street—I didn't know whether this address was correct, nor where it was exactly.

And, of course, I didn't know whether Luiza had called and told whoever was there that I was on my way.

The suburb of Saint-Cloud was unlike the city. It was still unmistakably Paris, but it wasn't one of the twenty arrondissements. I wasn't in Kansas anymore.

Where the city has a consistency imposed by central planning 150 years ago and a density of humanity as a consequence of the price of land, this suburb—a former commune, which was once outside the city before it was subsumed by the urban sprawl—had more space and showed different priorities.

Gone were the broad boulevards, to be replaced by narrow streets with one lane to park and another to drive along. Gone were the wide sidewalks, to be replaced by narrow tracks flanking the road. Gone was the City of Light—there were just a few streetlights spilling their weak yellow light onto the rain-soaked ground below and making little difference to the darkness beyond the road. And where the buildings in the city were built at the edge of the sidewalk, here the residences were set back from the street. And between the sidewalk and each house, there was a wall and a front yard.

But it wasn't simply a wall and a front yard—this was a positive and concerted effort at privacy and separation. As I walked, I saw that the walls were, on the whole, low. But topping the walls were metal fences—sturdy metal fences with spikes on top and panels between the railings for privacy and to make them really difficult to climb.

Then immediately behind the wall/metal fence combination, people had planted in their front yards. Thick hedges, bushes, and trees spilled over the top of every metal fence. Every single one. If I stood back in the street I could see the top half of a house across the road, but when I got up close my vision was blocked by the undergrowth.

I walked half a block and climbed up on a low wall to see over the metal fence, straining to see through the undergrowth. With my head shaking the tree I stood under, all I did was cover myself in a small deluge as the tree let loose its load, dumping cold water over me. I walked another half block, periodically pulling myself up on walls and straining to see through the undergrowth what was on the other side. Occasionally, a house would be lit up, which would give me some indication of where I should be looking, but often all I saw was darkness.

A phone rang. Unfamiliar but close. It took me a moment or two to twig that it was Luiza's phone ringing. I pulled it out and looked at the screen: Beatriz.

"Hi."

"Oh Leathan, I'm glad you answered. I didn't know how else to reach you." Her voice was quiet, hurried. I continued walking as she talked, reaching an intersection. Doing my best impression of Beatriz, I kept Luiza's phone clamped to my ear and pulled out my own phone to check the map. Beatriz continued, "They're coming. They know where you are."

"How can they know where I am?" I asked. "I don't know where I am, so they can't know where I am. No, wait..." The map on my phone caught up—it was the street I wanted. "I know where I am."

Beatriz was getting impatient. "Leathan, they're coming."

"Who is *they*?" I asked.

"Matheus Santos and Henrique Teixeira. They're coming. They're angry—no, they're furious with you—and they've got guns."

Something made me smile as I headed down the street—another narrow road, more of a service passage between the generous tracts of land attached to each property, with steel fences and dense undergrowth providing a green shield for each home. I wasn't sure why I was smiling; maybe something about the ridiculousness of the two men running around Paris with guns. And it wasn't as if there was anyone to smile at—I had been here for about five minutes and I'd yet to see a single human being.

"They don't know where I am," I said, still smiling at their ridiculousness.

"They found Luiza," said Beatriz. "We came back to the hotel, and she was coming up in the elevator—I think she was going to get some things and run. I don't know what she told them, but..."

I hung up before she could finish her sentence.

twenty-two

The address was accurate—the street existed, and the house number on the gatepost also tallied with the scrap of paper I had recovered from Luiza.

But while it was a genuine address, that didn't tell me whether Guilherme was there, nor whether anyone involved in his disappearance was there.

The property was like the others in the street—a steel fence with dense foliage behind. The only reason I was sure there was a building beyond the thicket was the few lights that peeped through.

A double gate—large, imposing, big enough for a small truck with a careful driver—offered access to the property, but it was higher than the steel fence. Higher than my eye line and where the fences were set atop a low wall, there was nothing to stand on to give me some lift to see over the gate, and even though I hadn't seen anyone on the streets of Saint-Cloud, I wasn't about to start jumping up and down.

I wasn't going to do anything to draw attention to myself while I was unsure about whether Guilherme was in the house.

I walked down the street to the next house. Another thicket, and more lights pushed through. Up the street to the other immediate neighbor, and either the thicket was incredibly dense or the lights weren't switched on. But there was a streetlight by the fence. It wasn't ideal to climb over the fence, but it would be possible. However, it would be faster to climb the shaped shaft of the light than it would be to try to negotiate the spiked fence without aid.

I still hadn't seen anyone—walking or driving—since I had arrived in Saint-Cloud, but that still didn't stop me looking before I raised myself on the lamppost. Another look and I put one foot onto the fence—twisting my ankle to fit my toes between two spikes.

The lamppost was good to get up, but there was nothing to climb down on the other side. There was a thicket of greenery, but I couldn't find a solid branch in the wet vegetation. On the plus side, I hadn't heard any dogs barking.

Across the end of the street I saw headlights move, and the rumble of an engine became louder. The first sound since the cab had driven off. If the car was going to turn into this street, then I suspected the first thing the driver would see would be me, standing like a ballerina with his tiptoe on a steel fence and a lamppost for balance.

I couldn't figure an innocent explanation I could offer the police, so I pushed from the lamp and let myself fall into the thicket, taking on faith that I would be able to grab a branch to slow my descent.

I didn't find a branch; I just ripped my hands as vegetation slid through my palms. But I was far enough into the thicket and the thicket was dense enough to counteract some of the gravitational forces, so when I hit the mud—it being comparatively springy with all the moisture it contained— my landing was softer than I deserved. Wet. Muddy. Cold. But nothing was broken, and nothing was bruised.

I rolled back into the thicket, desperate for some cover, but as I came to a stop—now covered in more mud plus some leaves—my concern seemed misplaced. Unless this tract of land had a very secretive alarm, no one had noticed my arrival, and the house that I could now clearly see had no lights illuminated.

I stood and headed toward the fence separating the two properties, again finding a thicket of greenery enclosing along the side with the fence formally demarcating the boundary. I pushed myself deep into the new thicket, not managing to pass, but hiding myself from view on either side while getting a reasonable view over the fence.

I soon forgot my caution about being on private land— my attention was drawn to next door.

There was a car—a dark blue Toyota Prius—on the drive and backed up to the front door, which was open like the car's back. There were three men—two in their twenties and a third aging hippie, maybe around sixty, but with the sun damage his skin had suffered, he could have been anything between forty and eighty. The three were going into and out of the house and loading the back of the car. There was a lot of semi-panicked talking and calling between the three—the chosen language was English, although none was a native speaker.

There was no sign of a kid, or anyone else for that matter.

And there was no sign that these guys were kidnappers—they could just be three guys loading a Toyota Prius.

I pulled out Luiza Pérez's phone and started flicking through the call log. I tried a number. It rang, then went through to voicemail. A second number. Ringing, then someone answered—female, older, speaking a language I didn't speak.

I tried a third number. It began to ring in my ear, and somewhere toward the house I was watching I heard a phone begin to ring. The older hippie guy came out of the house, trying to hold the box he was carrying in one hand as he stuffed his other hand into a pocket. He dropped the box, spat out a curse, and then pulled out his phone. "Luiza?" he asked, a hint of confusion in his voice.

I hung up.

It was time to get around the back and see if I could see Guilherme.

twenty-three

Around the back, I slipped over the fence, into the backyard of the building where I suspected Guilherme was being held.

The place was low and squat, spreading like a middle-aged guy whose diet consisted of hamburgers, soda, and ice cream and whose longest walk was to the car in the drive. At the back of the house there were no lights, but light spilled through from the front of the house.

And I couldn't see Guilherme or anything that suggested Guilherme might be present.

It was time to try another angle. Perhaps I could come in through the front gate. Or maybe it was time to call the cops.

I made my way back over the fence to the neighboring house, which from every angle seemed to be unoccupied. Across the front yard I pushed through the undergrowth, stopping when I reached the steel fence. If there was anyone on the other side, a head slowly raised above a steel fence would be far less obvious than jumping over.

The road was on a hill. At the top of the hill was a vehicle that hadn't been there when I climbed over the fence. A boxy blue Mercedes SUV, parked badly. Where every other car was parked forming a single row, which allowed traffic to pass in the other lane, the Mercedes was parked—more dumped—at an angle to block the entire street.

The driver and his passenger stepped out and had a brief conversation across the roof of the vehicle.

I recognized both men—Gabriela Carvalho's personal security detail, Matheus Santos, and his number two, Henrique Teixeira. I levered myself over the steel fence and onto the sidewalk.

I had passed three houses before they noticed my approach. It was Henrique who nodded to the other man—they said nothing and waited for me to reach them. I was about five feet away when Matheus pulled his pistol. "Where's the kid?"

"I don't know," I said, pleased that he had chosen to speak English. "Where did you leave him? Maybe I can help you search."

Santos did something with his gun—it gave a metallic click, which I'm sure was meant to scare me. Trouble is, I don't understand guns, so I didn't know what he did, and it didn't concern me any more than knowing that a man I didn't trust was waving a gun in my general direction. Waving a gun when there was potentially a kid around—a kid whose sense of personal safety might not be as well-honed as an adult's.

I did the calculation in my head: Was it safer to have an unstable angry man with a gun near where I suspected the kid was, or was it better to lie to the Brazilian security operative? "You can wave your guns all you like—shooting me isn't going to make me know where the kid is. Shooting me will make me go 'ouch'; it won't give me second sight."

"Where is Guilherme?" asked Santos. Something hard poked me in the back. I assumed it was Teixeira with a gun, trying to show me he was just as mean and tough as his boss.

"I don't know," I said, and it was true—I didn't actually know where the kid was. I suspected, but technically I did not know.

"That's not what we heard," said Teixeira behind me.

"If I knew where Guilherme was, then I'd be with him," I said. "So far, all I've got is this street, and there are quite a few houses. You can bang on the doors and ask if they've got a kidnapped child in here, but I'm not sure that it'll turn out like you hope."

Santos looked over my shoulder. I suspected he and Teixeira were trying to decide what to do next, holding a conversation without using words.

"And what do you mean, that's not what you heard?" I asked, throwing my head backward as if to indicate I was referencing the younger man's assertion.

More looks over my shoulder.

"I'll let you in on a secret," I said, preparing to tell the two something that wasn't even vaguely secret. "You've been played by the person who is responsible for the kid being snatched. Think about it—if Guilherme is here and I know where he is, then why would I tell that to Luiza?" I paused, then added emphasis. "How else could she know about this address unless she's involved?"

Another look over my shoulder. Santos raised his eyebrows, questioning the other man. A tilt of the head to respond to the reply, and then his gaze returned to me.

"Can we put the guns away now?" I asked. "You're only going to hurt yourselves and Guilherme."

Santos hesitated; then, chagrined, he complied.

"Where's Pierre Alvaréz?" I asked.

"Got the shits," said the younger man behind me.

"And I'm guessing he got the shits immediately after Luiza Pérez blurted out where the kid is being held?"

The look between the two answered my question.

"Can I summarize the situation?" I said, and continued before receiving a response to my rhetorical question. "Two people within your close circle have, shall we say, divided loyalties. That's the close circle where you work every day and where you are responsible for security. And those two people have created this problem."

I waited.

When they didn't say anything, I pushed again. "Two people have created this problem and yet you point a gun at me."

There was a glance between the two. A realization as the possibility struck.

"I think, gentlemen, that it's time we called the police."

twenty-four

At the other end of the street—the foot of the hill—a vehicle pulled up. I wouldn't normally have paid attention, but it was driven hard and it skidded to a halt. Sure the blacktop was wet, but that lack of control was unnecessary and quite hard to achieve in a vehicle with anti-lock brakes—a feature that I was sure was fitted to every Land Cruiser.

The skid was enough to grab my attention.

It also grabbed the attention of Matheus Santos and Henrique Teixeira. Both had their pistols in their hand when I looked around.

"We don't want shooting," I said. "There's a kid."

Santos let off a shot in the direction of the black Land Cruiser. I guess he had a different opinion about the possible ramifications of discharging a handgun in a quiet, suburban, residential street at 8:30 in the evening.

The shots were loud, but the sound was different from the shots I'd heard before. Shots inside tend to be bright, and the initial impact lingers. But here, outside, in the damp, the shot was loud but dull—there was no reverberation, and the sound immediately faded.

Even at somewhat over fifty yards and in the low light, I recognized Sylvain Mercier immediately, and doubtless Jordan Roussel wouldn't be far behind. Mercier was out of the Land Cruiser and sprinting. His gun was pointed in our direction, and I heard the report as he pulled the trigger—more dull pops—but the bullets came nowhere near us.

The lack of accuracy was good—for me. I was comparatively safe with incompetents like these around. If they ever learned to shoot, then I'd be in trouble—but that was a problem for another day. At the moment my problem was that there were two pairs of men—one pair at each end of the street—unloading their guns with little caution and much testosterone-fueled anger. Halfway between the two was a house where I suspected seven-year-old Guilherme Carvalho was being held by kidnappers.

I might have been comparatively safe, but I wasn't stupid. I dived behind a car at the end of the row. A bullet hit a brick pillar across the road. It wasn't precision shooting—it was probably just a fluke—but it was enough to scare Gabriela's men, who retreated behind their Mercedes before they continued firing.

Along the street, behind the hedges, lights were coming on. Somewhere near to me there was a deep voice, followed by a higher-pitched, panicked voice calling the deeper voice back. A solid wood door shut.

I started moving down the row of cars, heading toward where I had seen the three guys loading the Toyota Prius.

A quick look: Mercier was moving up the street, coming up the hill. I ducked down and dropped to the other side of the rank of cars, moving farther down the street—toward Mercier. Toward where Guilherme might be.

Two shots down the hill and five shots returned up, then it went quiet. Mercier seemed to be retreating—or maybe he just needed to reload. I was within ten yards of the lamppost I had used to clamber over the steel fence. I dropped down another two cars and was level with the lamppost. Ducking between the cars, the lamp was one lane of blacktop and the width of the sidewalk away from me.

I calculated the odds and sprinted. As I reached the lamppost I heard shots from both sides—loosed with their customary incompetence and lack of care for any unintended consequences. The shaft of the lamp was slippery, but the knurled detail gave me some grip, and I lifted myself off the ground, getting my feet to the small foothold on the vertical shaft from where I had previously ballerina-stepped onto the fence.

At the foot of the street, Mercier shouted and started to run up the hill. One of the two at the top responded with a shot.

I jumped, launching myself as best I could toward the dense green undergrowth that had slowed my descent last time I passed.

One foot pushed firmly, the other slipped, and I found myself twisting as my head and torso passed over the fence, gravity beginning to take effect. My left calf hit a spike on the top of the steel fence, and there was a rip before my body hit the ground having not fully immersed in the green thicket I hoped would break my fall.

There was a shout on the other side of the fence as I pulled up my leg, wincing in pain and feeling my back and shoulders where I'd be bruised tomorrow.

Another shout on the other side of the fence—a different voice—moving right to left and up the hill. Then there was an additional shot. The source was close, but the bullet went away from me. I rolled into the undergrowth and half-stumbled, half-righted myself. I didn't want to know what was happening and I didn't want to be close to guns being fired.

From the house where the Toyota Prius was being loaded, there was a low-pitched squeal, the sound of metal turning on metal. A wooden door slammed, then car doors. I ran, feeling the pain in my calf, and pushed myself through the thicket separating the houses. My eyes were drawn to the red taillights as the Prius slipped off the driveway, through the now open gates, and into the street, turning right and heading downhill.

There was another shout, a shot, and then running feet. Sylvain Mercier and Jordan Roussel both crossed in front of the open gate, sprinting after the dark blue Toyota.

twenty-five

There were shots and shouting in the road. The latest noise came from up the hill and seemed to be directed toward where the Prius had driven and where Sylvain Mercier had run.

I ignored the pain and clambered over the fence. The front of the squat house where the Prius had been parked was still lit inside, but the front door was now shut. I tried the bell, then hefted the door with my shoulder.

The door was stronger than my shoulder. And the door hadn't just made a stupid move by running between badly aimed bullets and then broken its fall as it jumped from a lamppost. If there was going to be a fight between the door and my shoulder, then tonight—and given my lack of time—the door was going to win.

I needed another option and started clambering over the back gate. I hadn't paid attention to the doors at the back, but people tend to put bigger locks and heftier doors at the front of their house. Less so around the back.

I dropped from the gate and landed heavily, feeling the kind of pain that told me I had done enough for one day. The body has physical limits, and I was getting close to mine.

A small, paved path led around the side of the house, bringing me to the backyard. The back rooms were still unlit, but light from the front of the house pushed its way back, and a weak glow found its way into the backyard.

I tried the first door—the kitchen door—and cursed to myself. The door was unlocked. I could have just walked in half an hour ago.

I stepped into the kitchen, quietly closed the door behind me, and stood still, listening.

The house was silent. There was no creaking. No groaning as the heating worked. No noise from the street. Just silence.

Silence, and my fingerprints on the back door handle.

I crossed the room and clicked on the lights with my elbow. The brightness was blinding, and I took a few moments as I felt the blood rushing in my eyes while my irises adjusted to the change.

A granite counter followed two sides of the kitchen, and in the opposite corner there was a table. I picked up a cloth on the counter and wiped the door handle—inside and out—then turned to face the room.

Where the counter ran out, there was a trashcan with a flip-up lid. The can was full of trash spilling out the top and forcing the lid permanently open. Around the foot of the trashcan, more rubbish had been stacked.

The visible trash seemed to mostly consist of wrappers from microwave food, empty soda cans, and boxes for kids' toys.

There were two chairs at the table, both on the same side, one stacked with cushions. The table was spread with paper. There was a large art pad, the page size twice or three times the size of regular letter paper. Someone had been drawing, and once each picture was complete it was neatly removed from the pad and the next picture commenced.

Some pictures were drawn in felt-tip pen. Some were drawn with crayons. Others were drawn with chalk. And a few were drawn with artists' pastels. I could be certain about the tools used for the pictures because the art materials—all new, all probably only opened today—were there on the table.

"Minha mamae por Guilherme," said the first picture. It was crude, but I wasn't going to ding a seven-year-old for lack of artistic practice. Crude, but I got that this was Gabriela Carvalho. I also got that Guilherme sees his mother as a woman who smiles.

I moved the picture and looked at the one underneath. Another picture of Gabriela. Again smiling, and I noticed, flicking back to the first, also with gold jewelry, although between the first and second the jewels had changed.

The kid had been busy today. There were at least forty pictures with a range of subjects—soccer, airplanes, mountains, animals—but the predominant subject for at least one quarter of the pictures was Gabriela, and while I'm no child psychologist, the pictures were drawn by an artist who loved his subject.

The sound of a siren at a distance broke my concentration.

I could take a chance they were going somewhere else. I could take a chance that I was hearing an ambulance or fire siren, but why risk it? Since I'd left the taxi in Saint-Cloud, I'd only seen three other vehicles, and one of them was the departing Prius. I picked up two pictures of Gabriela and folded them into my jacket pocket, then dashed around the house. I wouldn't say I'd checked every tiny hidey-hole, but I looked where I could. There was no Guilherme. There was no one else, so I headed to the front door, opening it with the cloth I still carried.

"I knew you were here," said Matheus Santos. "Lights going on all over."

And he was right—I had switched on the lights as I looked around the house—but now the siren was getting louder and coming closer.

"Let's go," I said, pushing past him.

"No," said the security man. "I want to..."

"Whatever you want, you can't have. Unless you want to be arrested and to explain that gun in your pocket."

He snorted and pushed past me.

"He's not there," I said. Santos stopped in the hallway and spun. "Guilherme's not there," I repeated to make sure the other man was clear who I was talking about. "He was here, but now he isn't."

"What do you mean?" Suddenly the gun was out again, and Santos was reaching forward, pushing me against a wall and gripping me by my throat.

"I mean Guilherme was here, but now he isn't—it's not a difficult concept, Matheus." He released his grip on my throat and stepped away. The gun was still in his hand. "He's gone because of you."

Santos returned his attention to me—the gun now pointing directly.

"The kid isn't gone due to a coincidence—we're talking cause and effect. Cause: You made a noise. Effect: Whoever had him got spooked and drove off. We had a lead—we no longer have a lead. There was no reason to have a gun battle on the streets—there was no reason to have a gun battle with people who we know don't have the kid."

The security man returned his gun to its holster under his arm.

"The kid will probably be out of the country by the time you get back to the hotel—and he'll certainly be gone by morning. France has porous borders and a huge sea coast."

The twitch on his face told me he knew that what I was suggesting was possible—if not likely—and he was figuring how he would explain to Gabriela.

"If you want to do the sensible thing, wait for the cops." I indicated the siren, which was probably two or three streets away. "Tell the cops—they can close ports and borders, or if not close, at least get people looking."

He shook his head. "You're coming with me."

twenty-six

Henrique Teixeira had moved the boxy Mercedes SUV down to the gate and was waiting for us with the engine running. Matheus Santos had decided to leave the house where Guilherme had been held, but not before deciding that my presence was required to help explain the situation to Gabriela.

The journey back was slow. Despite being well past the rush hour—my phone said 9:00 PM when we reached the hotel—the roads were busy, and with the now heavy rain, the traffic had slowed. Drivers seemed to be double- and then triple-checking at each junction. An abundance of caution seemed to be how they would proceed.

We completed the journey in silence.

Beatriz Marques opened the door for me and Santos—Teixeira had gone to park the SUV. The phone was missing from her ear, and she seemed to sense our mood, mirroring our silence as we trailed into the reception room with a view over the city.

Santos motioned to the sofa. It was the first direct communication between us since we had left Saint-Cloud.

I sat and looked back at Gabriela's two employees. They were silent, but something was passing between them. "Where's Gabriela?" I asked.

"The dinner meeting is overrunning," said Beatriz. "Pierre has disappeared, so I've called Henrique to go and wait for her."

The silence slipped back over the room, and the two employees continued their discussion, carried out through glances and contorted facial expressions.

"Is there something I should know?"

"No."

"Yes."

Santos with the negative. Marques with the positive.

"So maybe," I said. "Beatriz, what do you think I should know?"

She nodded defiantly at Santos and then turned to me. "There was a demand." She hesitated. "They got in touch."

I sighed. I felt no victory. I felt no joy. But somehow I suspected I was about to learn more about the true aims of the kidnappers who had been aided by Luiza Pérez. "What do they want?"

Santos replied. "They're terrorists."

Beatriz frowned. It was the kind of frown that a mother might give if her son used a strong word. "We don't know that they're terrorists, Matheus. We know they have an ecological agenda...."

Before Santos could argue, I cut across. "What do they want?"

"A complete change in corporate policy," said Beatriz. "They want the company to end all mining in Brazil and to close all other mining projects around the globe where there is any environmental impact."

"You can't mine without environmental impact," said Santos. "That's the point of mining—to make an impact."

Beatriz signaled him quiet. "The demand is not practical. The implications are significant—large-scale unemployment for all our miners, financial collapse for the company, which naturally would have implications for our shareholders, and the timescale in which a decision was required was... ridiculous."

"What was the demand?" I asked softly.

"That Gabriela make the announcement of the change of corporate policy this afternoon. At the conference."

A quiet fell over the room again.

It seemed to be my role to break the uneasy silences. "You knew," I began. "When I turned up at the conference center this afternoon, you knew this."

Beatriz flushed; Matheus stared at the carpet. The assistant offered a few words. "That's why we all thought you were wrong about Pierre and Luiza, and the two groups. We had a demand."

"Pierre and Luiza have gone now? And you get my point that there were two groups—one didn't have the kid but had asked for money, and when that failed, they tried to find the kid and grab him so they could demand a ransom. The other—"

"You don't always get all these things right the first time," said Santos, a scolded child who was still staring at the carpet.

"Call the police," I said. "They can get borders watched. They have the manpower to handle this sort of thing."

"We don't know—" began Beatriz.

"We do know. We know where he was when this idiot here pulled out his gun and scared the kidnappers," I said, indicating Santos. Santos didn't dissent.

"How?" asked the assistant. "How do we know?"

I pulled out the two pictures I had recovered from the kitchen in the house in Saint-Cloud, carefully unfolding the heavy drawing paper that showed what might be the last pieces of art completed by Guilherme Carvalho during his seven years of life.

Beatriz looked down over the two pictures of her employer. "It's his. That's what he draws. His mother, soccer, planes, and animals." She threw a glance over to Santos.

"I'll call her," he said, moving off into one of the side rooms and closing the door behind him.

twenty-seven

I wanted a beer.

I settled for a coffee when Beatriz offered. I somehow suspected that the beer room service would bring up would be disappointing—it didn't seem the kind of hotel that placed any value on serving the beer-drinker market. Added to which I wasn't quite ready to submit to the haze of alcohol I knew I would need to find when I tried to dull the thought of the stupidity of the people I had spent the day with.

Having placed the coffee on the low table in front of me, Beatriz Marques scuttled off. It seemed that without her phone clamped to her ear, connecting her with people demanding of her, she didn't know what to say or what to do. I wanted alcohol to blot out the world—she had a job that blotted out the world and didn't give her a hangover.

Or maybe Beatriz was reminded by my appearance—in short, wet and muddy—that I had been out, actively looking for Guilherme. Maybe she knew that if she engaged me in conversation I would repeat what I had already said several times: Guilherme was likely on his way to an airport, probably a small one, where he would be bundled onto a plane—which would be good for him since he liked planes, but bad for everyone else since the plane would likely be heading out of France, and wherever it was going, the price for the kid had just gone up. The conditions for his return had just become infinitely harder. He certainly wasn't in a place where one guy could walk in.

If I were Beatriz, I wouldn't talk to me. I wouldn't want to have me remind her that she was, in part, responsible for the situation the kid was in, so I too would have left the room. I too would have left me on my own with a cup of coffee.

A door on the side wall opened. Matheus Santos returned, closing the door behind him. He remained silent as he walked to the sofa next to mine, where he carefully lowered himself, sitting on the front edge of the seat.

He reached into his jacket pocket. His eyes flicked to me, checking he had my attention, before he pulled out a handful of bills. On the top was a €500 bill. Another flick of his eyes to check he still had my attention, and he peeled off the top bill, placing it carefully on the table, next to my coffee so I'd have to reach over the bill to take my next sip.

He took the next bill—another €500—and placed it slowly on top of the first. He continued the process until there were ten bills in the stack. Five thousand euros—the fee that had been suggested for me making the exchange. Five thousand euros to take the bag, give it to the nasty man, and bring back the kid.

He then took an eleventh bill, placing it on top of the stack, but perpendicular. He followed that bill with another nine bills, stopping when the combined stack was worth twice my fee. "There's a bonus," said Santos. "Gabriela would like to acknowledge in a practical way that what you did was beyond the scope of what we initially asked you to do. She would also like to show that she is grateful for your work today."

I reached forward, picked up the saucer on which my coffee cup stood, and moved it to the side, leaving the stack of bills untouched.

Matheus Santos pointed up and down at me, as if indicating my appearance. "If you have any injury, then please forward the bills to us. We will meet the payment."

I took a sip of coffee, careful to ensure Santos saw I wasn't touching the stack of cash.

Santos pointed to the cash. "You did good work. Good work deserves good money."

I ignored the cash and took another sip, returning the cup to its saucer. I wanted to ask him whether he had run off the bills on a photocopier, but now was not the time—I had a bigger point to make.

"Pick up the money, Leathan."

I gave a small, single shake of my head.

Santos cocked his head, questioning.

"I'm not going to be paid to fail. I'm not going to take your money—that would mean I agree that what went on today was good...sensible, smart...right.... If I'd got to the kid, then I'd take your money, but as it stands, you're paying me to say that what went on today is alright. And it wasn't alright—it was pretty much the dictionary definition of not alright. All you did was put the kid at risk, and with each turn you added more risk."

"You did good work, Leathan. You should be paid for that."

"Are you not understanding? Do I need to say it in another language to be clearer?" I asked. "I failed in the basic task of getting the kid back."

"Then come and help us look for him. Gabriela wants us to find Luiza and Pierre—they know more, and there must be consequences for their actions."

I sighed and flopped back into the sofa. "I don't doubt that those two know quite a lot. You will remember that it was me who suggested they were involved. But you're missing the point."

Santos raised his eyebrows but said nothing.

"There's a missing kid—Guilherme is still missing. Forty-five minutes ago he was in Saint-Cloud. Now he could be anywhere, but my best guess is he's within a forty-five-minute driving radius of Saint-Cloud. Within the next hour he could be out of the country. And even if the guys in the Prius are driving because an eco-car is better than a plane, they could have him into Belgium, Germany, Switzerland, Italy, or Spain by midnight. By morning it could be Turkey, Norway, Russia.... If they go for the coast, then by morning he could be in the middle of the Atlantic."

Santos still said nothing.

"Don't you get it? It's not something that I can fix anymore. It's not something that the two of us can fix. It's not something that ten of us can fix. It needs borders closed—as much as we can close borders. It need police checking. It needs ports and airports alerted. It needs pictures in the press."

Santos still said nothing, but his head was shaking—more of a vibration than a full shake. Enough to convey his disagreement, or more likely Gabriela's disagreement.

I drained my coffee cup and then reached into my pocket and pulled out a phone. "Luiza's phone," I said, placing it as a weight to hold down the stack of ten thousand euros Santos had placed on the table. "The logs might give you something, but I'm not going to join the search for the wrong people. I'm not going to say it's alright to use guns before brains."

I stood and left.

As I walked out of the hotel's marbled lobby, it was raining. The rain would only serve to clean me up a bit as I walked to a café where I could find enough beer to help me forget Guilherme Carvalho.

Note from the Author

I hope you enjoyed this book. If you want to know more about me and my books, then join my readers' group.

When you join, I'll send you my introductory library and add you to my readers' group mailing list. Every month I'll send you my communiqué, Simon Says. This includes news about my books, special offers, and extracts, together with a few pieces I think you may find interesting.

Join my readers' group and get your free books here: simoncann.com/readers.

Other books by the Author

Be sure to check out Simon's latest books at: simoncann.com.

The Leathan Wilkey series

Clementina

Leathan Wilkey faces up to the man who is menacing Clementina as a threat against her father.

Diplomatic Baggage

Leathan Wilkey thinks he has been framed for murder by the victim's father.

The Camera

Leathan Wilkey doesn't know who murdered his friend—or why she was murdered—but he will remain tormented until he brings about some sort of justice for her.

The Boniface series

The Murder of Henry VIII

When the author he is representing is murdered, Boniface realizes the job demands more than he expected. And when the man he is talking with is shot, Boniface runs.

Pollute the Poor

The first Boniface knows about the dead body in the next room is when he is arrested for murder.

Tattoo Your Name on My Heart

When his client's wife disappears, Boniface uncovers the secret she has been keeping from her husband.

About the Author

Simon Cann is the author of the Boniface, Montbretia Armstrong, and Leathan Wilkey books.

In addition to his fiction, Simon has written a range of music-related and business-related books, including the *How to Make a Noise* series, the most widely ready series about synthesizer sound programming, and *Made it in China*, about entrepreneurs building businesses in China. He has also worked as a ghostwriter on a number of books.

Before turning full-time to writing, Simon worked as a management consultant, where his clients included aeronautical, pharmaceutical, defense, financial services, chemical, entertainment, and broadcasting companies.

He lives in London.

You can find more about Simon at his website: simoncann.com.